A Cup of
Cold Water

A Cup of
Cold Water

The Compassion of Nurse Edith Cavell

Christine Farenhorst

PUBLISHING
P.O. BOX 817 • PHILLIPSBURG • NEW JERSEY 08865-0817

Map by Stephen Mitchell

Printed in the United States of America

Library of Congress Cataloging-in-Publication Data

Farenhorst, Christine, 1948–
  A cup of cold water : the compassion of nurse Edith Cavell / Christine Farenhorst.
    p. cm. — (Chosen daughters)
  Summary: Born in 1865 to an English vicar and his wife, Edith becomes a governess, then at the age of thirty a nurse, opening a nursing school in Belgium and serving there during World War I, when her compassion leads to her arrest for aiding the enemy.
  Includes historical notes, glossary, timeline, and bibliographical references.
  ISBN-13: 978-1-59638-026-4 (pbk.)
    1. Cavell, Edith, 1865–1915—Juvenile fiction. [1. Cavell, Edith, 1865–1915—Fiction. 2. Christian life—Fiction. 3. Nurses—Fiction. 4. World War, 1914–1918—Belgium—Fiction. 5. Great Britain—History—Victoria, 1837–1901—Fiction. 6. Belgium—History—1914–1918—Fiction.] I. Title.
  PZ7.F22297Cup 2007
  [Fic]—dc22

                                                                                2007015546

To Emberlee Kristin Koning,
Elineke Johanna Wilkinson,
Charity Larissa Bylsma,
Karina Rachel Farenhorst,
and Melissa Johanna Farenhorst—
all women who would not hesitate to offer a cup of cold
water to anyone in the name of Christ.
And to Betty Clapham,
who loves her neighbors as herself.

I Am a Gift

All that the Father gives Me will come to Me, and the one who comes to Me I will by no means cast out. For I have come down from heaven, not to do My own will, but the will of Him who sent Me. This is the will of the Father who sent Me, that of all He has given Me I should lose nothing, but should raise it up at the last day. (John 6:37–39 NKJV)

I am a gift, and He Who gave
Wrapped me secure with broken bread
And sacrificial wine-red thread,
I am a gift.

I am within my Giver's will
And given, come. A masterpiece
Whose standard value won't decrease,
I am within.

A keepsake I, who never shall
Be driven out, become obscure,
Until the final day endure,
I am beloved.

I'll not be lost or buried deep,
Forgotten in some earth-filled place
Where time will rot and hours efface,
I'll not be lost.

I shall be raised! For death has been
Quite swallowed up in victory,
And clothed with immortality
I shall be raised!

I am a gift, and He Who gave
Wrapped me secure with broken bread,
And sacrificial wine-red thread.
I am a gift.

Christine Farenhorst

CONTENTS

ACKNOWLEDGMENTS

I thank my husband, Anco, for encouraging me to write, for correcting dangling participles and misplaced prepositions, and for loving me! I also thank Melissa Farenhorst, who read through a portion of the manuscript while holidaying on the shores of Dog Lake and who heartened me with wonderful smiles while she could have gone swimming. As well, a hug for Claire Bedard, who spent a great deal of time going through the French portion of the text. And a compliment of perseverance for Karen Teeter at the Owen Sound Library, who continually supplied me with interlibrary loan material.

And I thank my Father in heaven for giving me the opportunity to write. May His name be praised.

Prologue: The Beginning

1860

Two women alighted from a horse-drawn omnibus at the corner of a small intersection in Islington, London. Gingerly stepping down, they stood for a moment as the clumsy contraption noisily rolled away.

"Is this the parish of St. Mark's, Mother?"

The daughter, aged sixteen or seventeen summers, looked about curiously. Her mother, a lady of some fifty years, answered confidently as she turned right onto a narrow lane.

"Yes, I'm sure it is. I checked the directions several times."

"Do we have far to go?" the girl asked, as she lifted her black skirt to follow her mother.

"Not too far."

Gutters bordered the lane, and the refuse heaped in them gave off a rank, unpleasant smell. Here and there children played, and a beggar called out from an open doorway.

"A ha'penny—a ha'penny for my supper!"

Trailing the women as they walked past him, he began to whimper.

"A farthing, pretty ladies—a farthing for my supper."

The mother quickened her step, paying no mind at all, but the daughter surreptitiously threw glances over her shoulder, inwardly relieved when the man stopped calling.

"Ah, here is the street we are looking for," the matron said by and by as they approached another intersection.

Rather thickset, she slowed her fast pace, her dark bombazine dress rustling with the exertion. Quite breathless, a great sigh escaped her lips as they turned the corner.

"I knew you would find it directly, Mother!"

The girl, becoming more talkative with each step, rattled on.

"This is a much nicer and cleaner street. I do hope the curate is a gallant and a kind man. Whatever shall we do if he doesn't hire you?"

The mother stopped abruptly and faced her daughter.

"Louisa Sophia, where is your faith? Remember that we have never wanted for anything. Your father, rest his soul, has been gone only a few months, and it was perhaps not meet for us to venture out so soon, but . . . . "

Her voice began to quaver, and she proceeded no further, for the girl had taken her arm, gently placing a forefinger on her mother's lips.

"Hush! Oh, Mother, I did not mean to vex you by my thoughtless chatter. I am sorry. It is only that I wondered . . . that I thought . . . ."

"Never mind, child. We'll discover what will happen soon enough."

The mother's anger ebbed as quickly as it had risen. They resumed their way, and Louisa glanced up at the grim outline of an almshouse. She shuddered involuntarily. Father had died of fever, typhoid fever the doctor had called it. He had been delirious for several days, and although she and Mother had nursed him devotedly, there had been no stopping death. And now they must manage without him.

"Here we are, child."

They halted in front of a house which, like its neighbors, was built of dull, brownish brick rising three stories high. The windows snubbed them with their shuttered eyes. A pieman down the street praised his wares loudly, and Louisa was suddenly reminded of the fact that she was ravenous.

"Perhaps he'll offer us tea," she said hopefully as her mother pulled the bell cord.

"You're to ask for nothing, child, and remember, address him as sir."

"Yes, Mother."

Louisa meekly fingered her jet beads and wished that she were wearing a green or yellow frock. Black made her feel homely, and surely sadness within could not be measured by the clothes one wore.

Inside the house, Frederick Cavell was having a particularly trying morning. The dining room table was stacked full of heavy books. Folios of notes lay on Sheraton chairs placed helter-skelter about the room. Candlesticks and boxes of this and that haphazardly filled the hallway and the rest of the house. Frederick Cavell, although an imposing man who could wield a hammer and strike a nail with accuracy and force, had not the gift of unpacking. Unfed, his stomach rumbled. The smell of last night's supper, which he had burned, made him avoid the kitchen. There was a stain on his collar, and the rumpled shirtsleeves sticking out from underneath a corduroy jacket were dirty.

Frederick Cavell was nearing thirty. A graduate in theology of King's College, London, he had afterwards gone abroad to Heidelberg, Germany, to further his study. Upon his return, he had been ordained as curate of St. Mark's in London. Although he was able to write fine sermons and sing in a splendid baritone voice, he bumbled about hopelessly in domestic affairs. When the bell rang, he tripped over the umbrella stand in a frantic effort to reach the door. Standing up and straightening his jacket, he sighed, fancying that he heard mice chewing in the walls. Then he opened the door.

"Good day, sir, I have come in answer to your advertisement."

A middle-aged woman stood on his doorstep. Behind her stocky figure, Frederick saw a young girl. As she peeped at him from behind her mother's back, she curtsied slightly and the grayest eyes he had ever seen—eyes as gray as the North Sea—looked deeply into Frederick's.

"Please come in," he said, bowing formally, "and please, please excuse the untidy condition of . . . of . . . well, of everything."

"My name is Mrs. Warming, sir, and I read your advertisement yesterday."

"Yes, well you will soon see that I am, indeed, in dire need of a housekeeper."

Mrs. Warming permitted herself a smile. Her bulk glided past Frederick and made its way through the hall, carefully noting the crooked coat rack, the fallen umbrella stand, and the stacks of boxes.

"Yes," she answered, "I think that you are."

Louisa followed her mother in and remained standing by the door. She studied, not the slapdash condition of the hall, but Frederick. He as well, drawn again and again to her eyes, seemed to forget for a moment why it was that they had come.

"Have you a room where we might discuss . . . " Mrs. Warming said, breaking the silence.

Frederick collected himself and abstractedly ran his hands through his black hair.

"Yes, please follow me. And again excuse my bad manners for not being able to allow you the luxury of sitting down in comfort. I have not, as yet, lit the fire in the fire grate. But then, it is a warm day."

Mrs. Warming nodded.

"It is of no consequence. I see you have many books. Have you also, sir, accommodations for a housekeeper?"

"Oh, yes. There are rooms upstairs. A bed-sitting room, I believe, is located on the second floor and should do someone nicely. When," he finished rather lamely, "things are cleaned up, that is."

"Might I see the kitchen?"

Frederick flushed, and his dark eyebrows knit together.

"Indeed. But it is not in good order, I'm afraid. I've only recently returned from the Continent, you see, and I am not used to . . . "

"I quite understand."

They followed Frederick down the hall, and rather shame-facedly, he opened another door. Mrs. Warming took in the greasy frying pans, the oil-spattered wall, and the soiled dishes with a measured glance. As she turned toward him, her bombazine dress rustled with authority.

"I am a gentlewoman in reduced circumstances, sir, and find myself in a position making it necessary to work to earn a living for myself and my daughter. I think," she continued, as she slowly extended her hand, "I think that we might be of some use to you, sir."

Frederick took her hand and shook it heartily.

"I am sorry to hear of your misfortune," he replied, "but glad that you see some hope for this muddle of . . . "

"We have a cat, sir," Louisa interjected, "and he . . . that is to say . . . "

She stopped, and Frederick smiled at her.

"I would also have advertised for a cat," he said, "but I didn't know until just a few minutes ago that I had mice."

Louisa's gray eyes sparkled into his, and for some inexplicable reason he felt capable of moving mountains.

Without much further ado, Mrs. Warming became Frederick Cavell's housekeeper. And during the course of that first year, finding Louisa both intelligent and charming, Frederick Cavell became the young woman's benefactor. He sent her away to school for two years to fill gaps in her education, and when she graduated, they were married. It was a love match.

I

SWARDESTON

Mrs. Cooke generally looked as if someone was pinching her. Her small mouth was consistently pursed, and her brown hair was pulled back so tightly that her forehead always seemed unhappy. But she had come highly recommended.

"I think she has some deep, dark secret hidden away in the nape of her neck," Louisa whispered to Frederick when they first visited Swardeston.

Frederick merely patted her hand without responding. The truth of it was that they could afford Mrs. Cooke. She fit nicely into their meager budget of three hundred pounds a year.

Swardeston was part of a circle of five small and rather poor parishes southwest of Norwich, the others being Intwood, Keswick, East Carleton, and Ketteringham. Swardeston, a hamlet of some three hundred people, possessed no vicarage and, consequently, Frederick and Louisa settled into a red-brick Georgian farmhouse on the village common. Sheltered in a bit of a hollow, the house stood alone. Great, majestic oaks surrounded it, trees that pointed their mighty fingers at the sky. Often when it stormed, small branches broke off and littered the yard. Frederick would then gather them into a pile behind the house to be burned.

"I'm no gardener," Mrs. Cooke told him the first time the wind raged about the house, her lips even more pursed than usual and her calloused hands pushed indignantly into her skirt pockets, "and I won't be cleaning up around outside and such."

But although she was no gardener, Mrs. Cooke was a jewel of a housekeeper. Her large and comfortable kitchen had a fireplace with a hob, and there was always a kettle simmering on it. She poured fragrant tea, baked wonderful ginger biscuits, cooked well, and kept the house spotless. In no time at all, Louisa doted on the woman and, in spite of her rather severe appearance, Mrs. Cooke was also fond of Louisa.

When Frederick accepted the living in Swardeston, Louisa's mother, Mrs. Warming, chose to stay in London. She had no desire, she told her daughter and son-in-law, to live in a small village, even though they assured her that Swardeston was only five miles south of the cathedral town of Norwich.

"And what would I be doing at my age walking five miles to get to civilization?" she asked in jest. "No, I prefer to stay where my friends are. I prefer to be where I can get to lots of shops and visit the markets. And young people like yourselves," she added, "should live alone."

There was no arguing with her, and, truth be told, Louisa rather enjoyed cutting loose the apron strings.

On an early morning in December 1865, the year the Civil War ended in the United States, Louisa became aware that her first child would soon make his or her appearance. It was going to be a freezing day. She knew it as soon as she woke up because her feet were cold. The wind whistled past the windowpanes, and she snuggled next to Frederick, curling her toes up against his warm legs. Frederick was always warm. She felt strange, a bit queasy and a trifle apprehensive. The baby was not due for another week; at least that is what they had thought. She wiggled her toes, and Frederick groaned, shifting a bit.

"Frederick?" she half whispered. The tiles on the roof rattled ominously. Feeling unprepared and immature, she wished that her mother were there.

"Frederick?" It was a cry now, and he answered in a voice thick with sleep.

"What's the matter? Are you cold?"

Putting his right arm around her, he pulled her close. But she didn't want him to touch her. The feeling of unease grew greater, and she pushed away the covers even though it was so cold that she could see her breath when she spoke.

"I think . . . I don't feel that well. Oh, Frederick!"

Abruptly awake, he was out of bed in an instant. In his hurry, he collided with the night table, and Louisa laughed in spite of herself. Ruefully rubbing his thigh, he grimaced at Louisa.

"Accidents will occur in the best-regulated families, as Dickens says."

Still smiling weakly, she leaned back against the pillows, pulling the covers back on. He sat down on the edge of the bed. "Are you feeling poorly, my dear? Is it . . . ? Is it . . . ?"

She nodded, and in an attempt at comfort, he awkwardly patted the round tummy bulging out the covers.

"Well, I'll get dressed and go for—"

"No, no," Louisa answered vehemently. "I don't want anyone just yet."

Turning over, she hid her face under the blankets. Uncertain, Frederick stood up and walked to the chair next to the dressing table. Quickly he began to put on his clothes, continually peering into the mirror to monitor his wife. Much to his consternation, she started breathing rather heavily after a few moments. Fumbling with his necktie, his fingers shook. Finally done, he walked over to the fire grate, kneeling to coax the coals into flame. Satisfied that the fire would keep going, he stood up, uneasily eyeing Louisa's form.

"I'll be back shortly, my dear. Just rest easy. I'll send Mrs. Cooke up with a nice cup of tea."

But Louisa kept her head under the covers, giving absolutely no indication that she had heard anything he had said. Closing the door quietly behind him, Frederick left.

There had been nothing, Frederick reflected fifteen minutes later as he walked down Swardeston's main road as quickly as he could, to prepare him for the birth of a child. He had not, in the two years that he had been vicar here, even baptized one. Five women in the parish had given birth, that was true, but all five babies had died. The thought made him lengthen his already long strides. There were very few people about. A farm laborer passed him, nodding curiously at the parson. The wind picked up in force, blowing Frederick's hat off, and for some moments he was totally preoccupied in extricating it from a hedge. He fancied there were people watching him from behind the cottage windows, laughing. They all probably knew, he thought, that he was on his way to fetch Annie

Hyde, the midwife; they all probably speculated that Louisa was in labor. Poor Louisa! He began to sweat even though the temperature was below freezing. What if Annie was not home? Pondering that possibility made his feet strike the cobblestones even more rapidly, and he wondered what course of action he would take if she was not. Unexpectedly his pace was broken and he found himself down flat on the rounded stones.

"Hello, Vicar."

The weather-beaten face of John Oldham, a day laborer at one of the local farms, grinned into his own. The man reeked of gin.

"John . . ."

"You have to watch where you're going, Vicar. I was having a bit of a rest here on the road. Figured this place was as good as any for a snooze."

"You've been drinking, John."

Frederick sat up. His trousers were covered in dirt, and his right knuckles were bleeding. John laughed out loud, stood up, and offered the vicar a solid, calloused hand. The road they were on, a road that struck off to Norwich, was rife with pubs—pubs that competed for the pay of many local workers.

"Aye, I've been drinking!"

Taking the man's hand, Frederick painfully stood up.

"You could have frozen to death sitting here, man! Why don't you go home? Besides, you shouldn't waste money on drink. Think of your poor wife and children in need of food and warm clothes."

"They'll always be needing that. Life's cold and hard, Vicar. Every now and then a man needs a pint to warm his innards."

Grinning, John lolled about before he began walking the wrong way. In God's strange providence he often makes mockery of plans. The upshot of it was that Frederick felt compelled to backtrack, and he saw John safely home before he resumed his way to Annie's house.

Annie lived in a small stone cottage just outside of Swardeston. Following a country lane and from there turning onto a well-worn mud path, Frederick breathed a sigh of relief when he finally reached her door. The small home stood among acres of plowed fields and grazing land. In the summer it was covered with honeysuckle and surrounded by roses, but on this cold December day it was a dreary, forsaken little place. Though Frederick knocked loudly and insistently, no one answered. After a few moments, he opened the door.

"Annie! Are you home? Annie!"

A cat rubbed about his ankles, and ashes glowed in the fire grate, but it was painfully obvious that there was no one about. Frederick stood for a few seconds, undecided. Then, turning around, he half-walked, half-ran to the nearest farmhouse and from there to another and from there back to Swardeston, for neither farmer could tell him where Annie might be.

It was almost midmorning by the time he returned to Swardeston. Jogging past the village common, much to the amusement of several women on their way to the greengrocers, he did not stop or raise his hat to greet them. Running across the gravel walkway toward the red brick house, he almost fell through the front door. Mrs. Cooke met him in the hallway.

"Oh, you're back, sir," she said as she took his coat and hat, her usually severe face wreathed in smiles.

"Yes, how is . . . ?"

"Mrs. Vicar, sir? She's fine, and so is the little one."

"The . . . the . . . the little one?"

"Yes, indeed. A fine little girl, sir. A bonny babe."

Frederick was not listening. He was already halfway up the stairs, his mud-spattered shoes leaving stains on the carpet. Mrs. Cooke tutted after him, but he paid no heed.

Louisa had her eyes closed when he walked in. Next to her, tucked into the hollow of the bed where he usually slept, was a little bundle. Kneeling down by the bed, he was about to touch his wife when a hand grasped his shoulder.

"Shh! She's worked hard, poor girl! Don't wake her!"

He turned and looked into the dark brown eyes of Annie Hyde.

"Annie?"

"Yes, it's myself," she whispered.

"How," he asked, standing up as softly as he could, "How did you—?"

She interrupted him, a twinkle in her eyes.

"Well, I was out for an early morning walk when I saw you take John Oldham by the arm. I supposed you went to take that drunkard home. Now why, I asked myself, would the vicar be out so early? So I decided to have a look-see at the house and sure enough, Mrs. Cooke was happy I came. And so," she added as an afterthought, "was Mrs. Vicar."

Louisa stirred, half-opening her eyes. Frederick knelt down again and kissed her. She ran her fingers through his thick, black hair. "You've a daughter, Frederick Cavell, a beautiful daughter."

He lifted his head and smiled at her. "It's Edith then, isn't it, my dear—Edith Louisa."

Louisa nodded, her eyes glowing with happiness. Getting up, he walked over to the dresser and took out a book. "I've a present for you," he said, handing her the volume.

"*Alice in Wonderland*," Louisa read out loud.

"Yes, it's just been published, and it's by a clergyman named Carroll, Lewis Carroll. He wrote it for the children of a friend, and I thought . . . well, maybe, when little Edith is a little older . . . well, that . . . "

Louisa smiled, put the book down on the blanket, and lifted up the swaddled baby lying next to her. Gingerly taking the bundle, he stared into big, wide-open, gray eyes.

"Hello, Edith Louisa, my firstborn child, my gift," he said. "May God bless you, and may you grow up to serve him in some special way."

2

THE NEW VICARAGE

For Edith's first birthday on December 4, 1866, she received a doll, beautifully dressed in a red, silk dress with mother-of-pearl buttons. Standing almost two feet high in leather kid boots, the toy contemplated the little girl with shining blue glass eyes. Rather in awe as she sat next to it on the front room floor, Edith touched the doll apprehensively.

"She's too small." Mrs. Cooke humphed disapprovingly as she looked askance at the gift.

Louisa laughed. "True, Mrs. Cooke," she answered, "but my mother must have saved a lot of half-pennies to have bought her such a doll. And I suppose that she will begin to play with it when she's good and ready."

"I'll get the tea," Mrs. Cooke said by way of answer and left the room.

The weather was cold and blustery, much like the day Edith had been born. Frederick, who had been reading the paper, got up and paced about after Mrs. Cooke left. Clearly there was something he wanted to say. Louisa waited patiently and continued her sewing.

"The truth of it is, Louisa," Frederick began a few minutes later, "the truth of it is that I've decided to spend the inheritance my father left me to build a vicarage for Swardeston."

He paused and looked at his wife to gauge her reaction. Face down, intent on working on a smock for Edith, she said nothing. Irritated, Frederick sat down again. But Louisa, after biting off the thread she was using, regarded her husband with a half-smiling, half-serious expression. Then, theatrically flinging out her arms, she stood up, dropping the sewing in the process.

"What!" she exclaimed in such a loud voice as to make Frederick look nervously toward the door. "No jewels, no furs, no footman or butler, and no expensive toys for little Edith?"

Edith, who had been fingering the new doll in a corner of the room, whimpered. Surprised by her mother's vehemence, she crawled toward Frederick. He picked her up, all the while formulating a reply.

"I cannot," he began as he dandled the child, repeating in an agitated manner, "I cannot . . ."

"I know, my dear," Louisa said soothingly.

She walked toward him and knelt down next to his chair. He sighed audibly, relieved that she had not been serious.

"It just goads me to anger," he said, "that back in London all matters are exaggerated. Champagne is served when barley water might do just as well. Men, even as ladies, change their clothes a great deal too often. And Mrs. Welsh, although I might add that she was a good enough friend to put me up while I settled my father's business, had so many servants she could probably populate Swardeston with them."

He paused, breathing heavily. Louisa patted his arm while baby Edith grabbed a handful of his black beard and pulled. Disentangling the child's fingers, Frederick continued.

"And the riots in Hyde Park were horrific. Women shouting and pushing for their right to vote."

"Well," Louisa said, "perhaps they should be given the vote. Mother and I knew a great many women who worked very hard for starvation wages. They had silly jobs like box making or tinting Christmas cards just so they could barely live. By the light of a stingy candle they . . . "

"I know, I know, Louisa," Frederick interposed, now soothing her in turn. "It's just that I despise riots. But I'm no snob, and you know it. I've never turned up my nose at . . . "

Edith grabbed her father's nose at this point and, having got a good hold on it, squeezed. The tension of the moment was gone. Louisa burst out laughing, and after gently disengaging Edith's hand, Frederick joined her. Edith squealed in delight as Frederick kissed his wife on the cheek.

"You are my Proverbs 31 wife, my mother in Israel," he said.

"Well," she replied, "the fact is that having a vicarage right next to the church, such as you have been proposing all along, is a good idea. I won't have to worry about you trudging half a mile in all kinds of weather to conduct services. And visitors will know, without having to ask, where to find the vicar."

Frederick smiled, relieved that she understood at least a portion of the thoughts that had crisscrossed his mind during the last few months.

"And how could I," he added, "how could I justify spending money on myself when so many here are poor. I often actually feel as if the clean and starched shirts I wear break faith with God when ragged, skin-and-bone children cross my path. For what do I have that was not given to me by our good and gracious God? And—"

"I understand," Louisa interrupted, "I really understand, Frederick! You needn't explain. And you understand too, don't you, my little dumpling?"

She chucked the baby under her chin, and Edith squealed again just as Mrs. Cooke knocked and came in with tea and biscuits.

"We'll be moving come summer, Mrs. Cooke," Louisa told the housekeeper, who unceremoniously deposited the tray on the table. "We're going to build a vicarage right next to the church."

Mrs. Cooke merely humphed by way of reply, keeping her thoughts to herself. And she humphed even louder when Frederick, in complete disregard of his position, dropped on all fours and began to play with Edith on the carpet. Growling like a bear, he tickled the delighted baby until she was weak with laughter.

As soon as the spring weather permitted, Frederick secured masons, carpenters, and a few young men who needed work. He laid out the grounds for the rectory so that the back yard of the manse adjoined the Swardeston church cemetery by way of a brick path. Not averse to helping, he worked with the men each day, encouraging and urging them forward. As a result, the vicarage was completed in record time. The Cavells moved in the fall of 1867 with Mrs. Cooke in tow.

"A grand, big house," the Swardeston villagers said, but then they smiled and thought of Mrs. Vicar, whom they loved and who was due to have another baby any day.

Florence was born in the new vicarage. Edith loved her wee sister, and a number of years later when little Lilian was born, she was very excited. In due time, Jack completed the Cavell family, and Mrs. Cooke was given to baking more and more cookies.

3

BLACKBERRY PIE

Rev. Cavell's study had a French window. Through it he could see a bit of the rose garden as well as the daisies, camellias, aspidistras, mimosas, and lilies, which Louisa together with Edith and Florence tended with care. Early mornings he often walked through the doors and strolled over the red-brick path in the flower garden toward the gap in the hedge leading to the churchyard cemetery. Here gigantic trees spread their branches. There were Irish yews, beech, and maples, as well as magnificent eucalyptus. Birds sang cheerily as they perched above the tombstones. Edith and Florence loved to play here. They spread napkins on the cement slabs and ate the little pasties and shortbread cookies that Mrs. Cooke sometimes allowed them to carry out for a picnic. Now and then Edith hid behind a tree and listened as her father conducted a funeral service. His deep and sonorous voice vibrated through the churchyard: *Man that is born of woman hath but a short time to live, and is full of misery. He cometh up, and is cut down, like a flower; he fleeth as it were a shadow, and never continueth in one stay.* Tears would come to the small child's eyes, even though she didn't quite understand why.

It was June, and Edith was eight. She and Florence had just finished shelling a basketful of peas for dinner. It was very hot, and in spite of the pokes both girls wore, the sweat ran down their necks in rivulets.

"Let's go and play by the church. It's cooler there in the shade," Edith said.

She had brought the peas inside to Mrs. Cooke and was carrying Wendy Warming, the doll her grandmother had given her for her first birthday. Wendy's clothes had torn over the years. As well, one of her eyes had fallen out, and her left arm was slightly dislocated. Even though Edith had poured some blue ink from her father's inkwell into the empty socket and her mother had doctored the arm, the doll was a far cry from what she had been. Nevertheless, Edith loved her very much and took her everywhere.

Florence willingly followed Edith to the churchyard. Lilian and baby Jack were sleeping, and Mother was taking a rest as well. Mrs. Cooke was busy in the kitchen, and Father was off visiting a parishioner.

"I know what we can do," Edith said pensively, regarding the gray church tower. "Let's play funeral and bury Wendy Warming."

"But we don't have a coffin," replied Florence, who was by no means ignorant about what went on during funerals.

"We can use the basket we put the peas in," Edith said, immediately turning around and running back to the house to get the container.

Mrs. Cooke had put the empty basket outside the kitchen door, and Edith picked it up, swinging it jauntily from her right arm as Wendy Warming dangled from her left. Just before the gap in the hedge, however, she stopped, thought for a moment, and turned around. She had forgotten one of the most essential elements needed for a funeral—a shovel. Picking up her mother's trowel from a nearby flower bed, she cheerfully skipped back to Florence, who was picking daisies at a nearby grave.

"We'll have to dig the hole first," she said, "and the sexton always does that. You can be the sexton, Florence."

"I don't want to be the sexton," Florence complained. She did not want to exchange her daisies for a trowel.

"You have to be the sexton. He's got dark hair, and so do you," Edith ordered.

Although Florence knew that there was no logic in her sister's statement, she had no desire to argue the point. Grudgingly she took the trowel from Edith's hand and half-heartedly began digging between two nearby tombstones. Edith laid Wendy Warming in the basket and covered her with yew leaves.

"Poor child," she whispered, "so soon taken from your beloved mother's arms."

"The ground's pretty hard, Edie."

Edith looked up to see her small sister meeting with very little success. She sighed and stood up.

"Very well then, I'll be the sexton," she said, "but you must weep over Wendy Warming."

Ten minutes later, Edith had a sizeable hole dug. She called Florence to come and bring the coffin with the child.

"Are you really going to put her in there, Edie?" Florence was aghast, staring at the small, black cavity with something akin to horror. "I see ants and worms and a spider," she added.

"Well, yes, of course," Edith replied, "because Wendy Warming is dead. And now you have to read, 'Dust you are and to dust you return.' Otherwise how could it be a real funeral, you silly goose?"

"What are you doing?"

Both girls turned. They had heard no one approach, and even now as they studied the graveyard they could see no one. Edith's heart pumped a little quicker. She had been a bit apprehensive about whether or not the real sexton, Bertie Dow, whose long, sinewy arms always made her shudder a bit, would be working in the cemetery that afternoon. Sometimes he clipped the hedge, and at other times he raked leaves when they were playing. She knew he might not approve of Wendy Warming's grave, small though it was. She searched the grave-yard again, but instead of Bertie Dow's rheumy gaze, she saw two pairs of small eyes peeping out from behind one of the massive eucalyptus trees.

"Can we play too?"

Breathing a sigh of relief, Edith grinned widely. The eyes belonged to Tom and Maggie Bentham, five-year-old twins who lived in the village. Smiling shyly, the twins stepped out from behind the tree. Jilly, their two-year-old sister, stood behind them.

"Sure you can play," she called out. "Come on over. We need some mourners. You'll just have to cry and—" She stopped, suddenly remembering that Father had buried Mrs. Bentham last month. Instinctively her eyes moved to the woman's grave. The earth was still fresh and turned up. Grass had barely sprouted around the flat tombstone. Tom's eyes sought out the place as well. He began to sniffle, and Maggie soon fol-lowed suit.

"I'm sorry," Edith began, but the twins, once they had begun the serious business of crying, could not stop. Edith looked at Florence, who shrugged. Jilly now began to cry as well, sitting down under the eucalyptus. Edith walked over and put an arm around Maggie's thin shoulders.

"Never mind," she consoled, adding for good measure, "your mother's in Abraham's bosom," but the words didn't help.

Underneath Maggie's plain brown frock, her shoulders continued to heave. And then, consumed with abject misery, she began to howl, all the while holding her brother's hand. Tom had pushed his face against the bark of the eucalyptus. His sobbing was not as loud as his sister's, but the sight of his shaking back brought tears to Edith's eyes.

"I know," she said. "I'll go round and ask Mrs. Cooke if we can have a picnic. I'm sure she'll let us have some cookies and a drink of lemonade."

Turning, she ran toward the gap in the hedge. The yellow poke, tied under her chin with ribbons, flew off her head and sailed behind her like a kite. She did not stop until she reached the kitchen.

Mrs. Cooke was sleeping. Her guttural snoring filled the doorway. It vibrated off the copper-bottomed pans hanging over the large cooking range and mingled with the sweet smell of a blackberry pie resting on the sill. Edith hesitated and watched. Mrs. Cooke sat in a high-backed chair. Her head leaned back; her mouth was wide open; and her white muslin fichu steadily rose up and down. Cheshire, the cat, was curled up by her feet. Edith knew for a fact that, when wakened from an afternoon nap, Mrs. Cooke's temper left a great deal to be desired. Humphs turned into harrumphs and chores were handed out. There was really no need to wake her and to ask permission for a picnic, Edith reasoned. Mrs. Cooke would be sure to say yes in any case, for wasn't Father always saying how they should help out the poor? The Benthams were very poor, to be sure! So why bother? Slowly tiptoeing over to the window, Edith reached up toward the sill. Her arms were just long enough. The pie was quite warm, but the checkered cloth beneath it sheltered her hands.

The Bentham children had stopped crying by the time she returned, and they were sitting in a small circle. Florence was rocking Wendy Warming, and everyone watched Edith as she came closer, carefully cradling the pie. She placed it in the center of the group, and Tom, Maggie, and Jilly ogled it. A sense of pride stirred within Edith, and she smiled.

"Eat as much as you like," she said magnanimously. "It'll make you feel better. But you'll have to use your fingers because I forgot the spoons."

The pie disappeared in no time. After that the little Benthams felt much better. It did not seem proper to continue with the doll's funeral arrangements, so Edith let Jilly hold Wendy Warming while they played hide-and-go-seek among the tombstones. And then, much later, everyone went home.

"Have you had a good day, Edith?" her father inquired at suppertime after he had said grace. He smiled at his oldest daughter, noting that she looked more like her mother each day. Reaching for his fork and knife, he contemplated the roast potatoes and the minted garden peas on the table with pleasure. Appreciatively breathing in their aroma, he repeated his question. "Well, daughter, how was your day?"

Edith's gray eyes met his for only a fraction of a second before they returned to her plate. "Fine, Father."

Her reply was subdued because she had just remembered that neither she nor Florence had bothered to tell either Mrs. Cooke or Mother about the pie—that wonderful blackberry pie that had so delighted the little Benthams and that had been devoured by them in the space of ten minutes. There was little doubt in Edith's mind that Mrs. Cooke intended to serve the pie as dessert. She swallowed audibly, hardly able to eat for fear of what was to come.

"I've just finished reading Darwin's latest book, Louisa. It's called *The Descent of Man*."

Frederick spoke with his fork halfway to his mouth, looking at Louisa as she helped Lilian put some food on her plate. Louisa nodded to show that she had heard him, and, satisfied with her attention, he continued.

"Foolish man, Darwin!"

"Why, Father?"

Edith asked in spite of the fact that the peas on her plate were beginning to look sickeningly like blackberries.

"Because, daughter," Frederick answered, "Darwin teaches a damnable doctrine. He does not believe that the Bible is the divine revelation or that Jesus is the Son of God."

Florence and Edith both stared at him, and he went on.

"Darwin wrote another book before either of you were born. It was called *Origin of Species*. In this book he said that all species—all plants and animals—were not created by the Word of God in six days but resulted naturally over millions of years. In short, girls, Darwin denied God as Creator. He was, therefore, and is, a liar. And liars such as Darwin," he finished, "unless they repent, go to hell."

"Sir?"

Mrs. Cooke was standing by the table, visibly agitated.

"My pie, Reverend Cavell," she pushed out, "my blackberry pie that I baked this morning . . . it's gone."

"Gone?" he answered, perplexed, "How can a pie be gone, Mrs. Cooke? It has no legs."

"It was cooling in the windowsill after lunch, sure as I'm standing here, and now it's gone."

"There have been one or two vagrants about," Frederick said. "But I hardly think they would be so bold as to come onto church property and steal a pie."

It was quiet for a moment or two.

"Have you seen anyone about this afternoon, Louisa?"

Louisa shrugged. "No, Frederick. But then I was in most of the afternoon. The baby was a little fussy, and I napped. But the girls . . . "

"Edith?"

"No, Father. After Florence and I shelled the peas for supper, we played in the cemetery, and the Bentham children came and . . . well, we played."

Edith dared not look at Florence, who had kicked her hard under the table. Her father sighed.

"Well, we must keep a lookout, and perhaps I should inform the constable."

Edith flushed. She opened her mouth but words would not come. No one had dessert, and Edith slept badly that night.

"Darwin was, and is," she heard her father repeat over and over in her mind, "a liar. And liars such as Darwin, unless they repent, go to hell."

4

CONSCIENCE STIRRED

As expenses increased with the birth of each new child, Frederick and Louisa Cavell realized that hiring a governess to educate their daughters and son was out of the question. Neither did they have enough money to send their children to a private school. Public school was out of the question, since most were primitive and lax. Consequently, Frederick was happy to take on the task of tutoring himself. And so it was that each morning, after prayers and breakfast, Edith presented herself in her father's study to read, write, and cipher.

"I noticed that you were late for prayers this morning, Edith."

Frederick's mild rebuke, given as he sat at his desk, demanded a response.

"Yes, Father," she said, "I slept rather badly and so I . . . I . . ."

"Mmm, yes," he responded, looking at her rather oddly. "And why do you suppose you slept badly?"

Edith blushed. The blackberry pie had caused nightmares.

"I . . . I . . . don't know, Father."

"What does God require in the eighth commandment, Edith?"

"To not steal, Father."

She looked down at her sturdy black shoes and her ribbed stockings as she answered. It was her father's habit, she knew, to quiz her on the commandments every now and then. But even so, his question hung about her like a dark mantle.

"That is well answered, my girl, and very quickly also. And," he went on, "what is required in the ninth commandment? Do you recall that one as well?"

"No false witness," she answered, eyes still cast down.

"Yes," he said, "and can my Edith come here now and sit on my knee for a moment?"

She hesitated before she slowly walked over to the desk and stood by her father's side. Frederick pushed his great chair back and patted his knees. Edith sat down. After a minute or so of quiet, she leaned back, snuggling her head against his tweed jacket. She closed her eyes and listened as her father spoke to her gently.

"I walked about in the cemetery early this morning. The blackbirds and thrushes were twittering away in the yew trees," he told her. "They swooped down every now and then to look for fat worms. And do you know one of them found? Not a worm, but a blackberry. The strange thing about this blackberry was that it was growing, not on a bush but on a plate—a pie plate."

Edith stiffened in her father's arms. "I'm sorry," she mumbled against his jacket. "I'm so sorry, Father."

"I am too," he said, pulling her up straight and looking her in the eye, "because it seems that my daughter, who can recite the Ten Commandments so beautifully from memory, can break them just as easily as she can say them."

"I didn't mean to, Father, honest, I didn't." Edith's voice trembled.

"I didn't think you did," he said, "but you know, Edith, when we disobey God's commandments, things just don't work well anymore. Stealing and lying destroy the peace that comes from knowing the Lord Jesus. It is almost, Edith," and he chucked her under the chin and made her look straight into his eyes again, "it is almost as if we choose death instead of life. Do you understand that, little one?"

She nodded and tears coursed down her cheeks. "Yes, Father."

"Now you must kneel, Edith. You must kneel and ask God's forgiveness."

She hopped off his knees and knelt down by her father's desk. He knelt down beside her. And they prayed together.

It was only after the prayer that she told her father about the Benthams.

"There are a great many hungry people in the world, Edith, and I'm glad that you have compassion for them. It's very important to have compassion, to feel love, and to have a desire to help others."

Edith nodded eagerly, happy to agree and happy that the awful burden of guilt had been taken away through confession.

Her father stood up and walked over to the window. He was a broad, tall man. His black beard curled about his chin, and he thoughtfully pulled at it with his right hand.

"What, little one," he said at length with his back toward her, "do you think we might do to help the Benthams and others like them?"

Edith came and stood next to him. The corners of her gray eyes crinkled in concentration.

"We might," she said after a while, "we might share some of our food with . . . with poor people."

"Fine," said her father, "that's a fine idea. Why don't you go and ask Mrs. Cooke to prepare this evening's meal with two extra people in mind."

"Two extra?"

"Exactly," her father smiled, "and then, right after grace tonight, we will fill two bowls with food, and you can take them over to Mr. and Mrs. Jacobs."

Mr. and Mrs. Jacobs were an elderly couple who were quite destitute. Mr. Jacobs was crippled, and Mrs. Jacobs took in washing. They had no children.

"After grace?" said Edith, "But I . . . then my food will get cold. Can't I do it . . . "

She stopped, confused, and looked up at her father.

"Would you rather not do it?" he asked.

"Well, yes, I would rather not," she faltered, "although I think it is right to do it . . . but I would rather not."

Her father chuckled. "That is the way of learning," he said. "And now, off you go to tell Mrs. Cooke so that we can get down to our reading."

5

A Cup of Cold Water

Edith was uncommonly talented in drawing. At night, she often pretended that her fingers were pencils, and she sketched onto a canvas of air before falling asleep. During the day, she drew on paper—dogs, cats, birds, and little children wearing large bonnets—with so much skill that her parents were amazed.

"There is no living in it for a girl," Frederick said to Louisa one evening after the children had all been put to bed. "But it will very likely be useful at some point in her life. Otherwise God would not have given her the gift. Besides, she has been given many other talents as well. Her understanding and grasp of history, mathematics, and literature are unusual for one who is only eleven."

Louisa nodded. "And she plays the piano very sweetly, too. But do you know what I really like about our oldest daughter?"

He shook his head, smiling as did so.

"Well," Louisa said softly, "she's such a mother. She's just such a dear when it comes to caring for the little ones. She reads to them hours on end from nursery books and draws pictures for them—not just to Florence, Lilian, and Jack, mind you, but to all the children from the neighborhood."

She stopped and yawned. Frederick stood up and, kneeling in front of the black horsehair chair where his wife was sitting, gently took one of her hands into his own. "That's because she has a good example in you, my dear."

Louisa blushed, and he reached up to kiss the tip of her nose.

"It's Sunday tomorrow. Best we be off to bed."

There was never any reason to be late for church. The sexton tolled the church bells, and at the first sound Mrs. Cavell, Edith, Florence, Lilian, and Jack—all in their Sunday best—made their way across the red-bricked footpath toward the cemetery. Crossing the gap in the hedge, they continued on the pathway through the graveyard toward the church.

It was February, and quite chilly out. Mrs. Cavell wore a white beaver bonnet and a cream-colored cloak. Her woolen skirt, spread out over hoops, made it appear as if she floated rather than walked. Edith and her siblings followed sedately, each carrying a Bible. The girls wore bonnets and cloaks. Their wide dresses did not allow them to press too close behind one another. Jack, last in the lineup, sported gray trousers, a silk shirt and tie, and an Eton collar. A long black jacket hid the slingshot in his back pocket. Mrs. Cavell, always the first to reach the church door, turned to make sure everyone was behind her. Satisfied, she sailed through and, keeping her gaze toward the chancel, headed for the front.

The Cavell pew was to the right of the pulpit, and from it they could see the villagers as they sat down. The blacksmith, the thatcher, the tailor, the cooper, the greengrocer, and the butcher: most of the families came, as well as the day laborers and the farmers. The church was peaceful, its whitewashed walls cleanly contrasting the dark, oak pews. Jack slid into the bench next to Edith, enthusiastically waving at a friend. She pulled down his arm, but he immediately began to play with the button of the pew door, which creaked horrifically at his touch. She pinched him, and he pulled the door shut.

Rev. Cavell, clad in a black gown, strode out of the vestry. Mounting the stone rood stairs, he entered the chancel. A hush fell over the congregation. Edith relaxed. Jack, now directly under his father's all-seeing eye, usually dared not act up when he was in the pulpit.

The Scripture passage, after the singing and the responsive reading, was from Matthew.

"For whomsoever shall give you a cup of water to drink in my name, because ye belong to Christ," Rev. Cavell read in his melodious voice, "verily I say unto you, he shall not lose his reward. And whosoever shall offend one of these little ones that believe in me, it is better for him that a millstone were hanged about his neck and he were cast into the sea."

"*A cup of water*," mused Edith, "*there was nothing better than a cup of cold water on a hot day—a day in which you'd worked hard in the garden, or a day . . .*"

"It is an honor," her father began his sermon, "a great honor to belong to Christ, but with belonging comes a good deal of responsibility. If you are joined to Christ, if you are his family, well then . . . then you are members of his body. And as such, you ought to be a refreshment to others . . ."

So I am a refreshment—I am a cup of water, thought Edith, and the thought made her smile. The truth was that when she, or her sisters, or Jack, took food to those who did not have as much, they usually did not take along a drink. Father, who carved the joint, put generous portions into basins with covers—basins that Mrs. Cooke brought into the dining room. They were always glad when the people they were instructed to go to did not live too far from home, because their own food often got cold. There was nothing worse than congealed gravy. Edith shuddered involuntarily.

"The relieving of Christ's poor must be done for his sake. He orders it. He commands it. The poor belong to Christ . . ."

Once, Edith recalled the time clearly, when she had walked over to the Widow Rigg's cottage with some food, she had been followed by a small, brown dog. She loved dogs and had stopped to pat it. Thin and friendly, the animal had licked her hand affectionately. She got to thinking that the Widow Rigg was as plump as a sausage and that the dog was as thin as a blade of grass. And before she knew it, she had opened the lid to the basin and had taken out a chunk of roast. Dropping it quickly, she did not dawdle to see whether or not the dog was eating. But a few moments later, the creature was at her heels once more. And, she recalled, she had lifted the lid a second time and had taken out a handful of greens and had dropped these also. Then she had set off in a run for the Widow Rigg's cottage, her right hand slippery with vegetable juice. The Widow Rigg had commented on the rather lean portion when she lifted the lid. But Edith hadn't minded. She didn't like the Widow Rigg.

"You must all remember also," Father's voice rang firm, "that at some point in your life, you might be at the receiving end. You might be reduced to such straits as to be glad of a cup of cold water. You might be sick, friendless, alone somewhere where you feel absolutely forsaken. But remember that you will never be so alone that God is not there . . . "

Edith tried to imagine what it would be like to feel alone and forsaken. She had never traveled farther than Lowestoft for summer holidays. Lowestoft was only fifteen miles from Swardeston, and it was not a forsaken place. On the contrary, there were always a great many people there—Uncle Edmund, Auntie, and Cousin Eddy, and surely there were hundreds of people on the beach. She loved playing with Eddy, who was not at all stuck-up about being a boy. And the North Sea was so vast. She loved the water, delighted in the great waves that rolled in, imagined who were on the ships in the distance, and licked the salt spray that fell on her tongue when she stuck it out. Mother and Father let her take her pastels and easel on holidays, and she could sit in the dunes for hours on end and sketch. Last year a seagull had filched one of her brushes. It had been really funny. Remembering the silly bird with the brush hanging from his beak made Edith softly laugh out loud. Jack punched her hard, and she suddenly recalled that she was in church. Ashamed, she hung her head.

" . . . every least degree of true faith, every expression of Christian kindness, is giving a cup of cold water and shall be accepted and rewarded by Christ. Do not forget it, brothers and sisters! Do not forget it! Whatever you do for one of your brothers and sisters, even for one of the least, you do for Christ."

Had it been an expression of Christian kindness to feed the stray dog? Edith was not sure. She could not really ask Father because then he would say, "Why do you ask, Edith?" Dogs were certainly not, she knew for a fact, the same as people. But they surely seemed nicer than some. She sighed deeply and let her gaze run over the people sideways across from the pew. The Widow Rigg sat close by. Her bonnet was green. The light shining through the yellow stained-glass windows danced on the empty pew next to her.

"As long as we are on this earth," Father said, and he gazed about the congregation thoughtfully, "as long as we are here, let us be sure that we are not self-righteous. Never say, my church in Swardeston is the best—or, my church in Swardeston is the purest example of the body of Christ on earth. Don't be hypocritical, friends! It does not do! Is it not better to leave such judgment to God? Is he not the best One to decide such matters? Let us follow what Jesus said, while we retain purity of doctrine, and let us reach out to all those who love the Lord Jesus. In doing so we might be instrumental in leading others to him."

The Widow Rigg shifted her position and suddenly looked straight at Edith, who was still contemplating both the light and the green bonnet—a bonnet that she found rather tawdry. Lifting her eyebrows slightly, the woman motioned that Edith should be paying attention to her father. Edith blushed and turned her head.

" . . . God threatens, yes, he threatens those who offend his little ones, those who grieve his children. This is no small threat, my congregation, no small threat at all. 'It were better,' says Jesus, 'that a heavy millstone be hanged around his neck, and he were cast into the sea.'"

Edith and Florence had been to the miller on the Wensun River. They had seen the millstones, for there was more than one. There was a top stone, drawn by a donkey. In the middle of the stone was a hole through which grain was fed so as to be crushed when the donkey pulled the stone over the one beneath it. *Imagine having such a stone around your neck and then falling into the North Sea! Have I grieved anyone?* Edith wondered. Without meaning to, her gaze returned to the Widow Rigg. There was no doubt about it; the woman was plump and then some. Perhaps not eating the roast and the greens had been good for her. After all, Mrs. Cooke often said that overeating led to stroke and to gout. But Mrs. Cooke also said gout was a rich man's disease, and Mrs. Rigg was a poor widow. Queen Victoria had gout. Queen Victoria was a rich widow. Indeed, she was very rich because she had just been proclaimed Empress of India. Edith sighed and fixed her eyes back on her father. India was far away. India sounded a bit like Intwood. There was a chance that tomorrow she might be able to go ice skating down by the ford at Intwood. She loved ice skating. And if Mother wouldn't let her go that far, maybe she and Florence could skate on the moat behind the rectory. Her feet felt the rhythm of the ice course through them, and she slid her right foot over the floor, smacking hard into the pew. Lilian threw her a frightened glance, and Edith sat up straight.

"Amen and amen."

After the final hymn, the offertory, and the prayers came the blessing. And Edith loved the blessing best of all.

"The grace of our Lord Jesus Christ, the love of God, and the communion of the Holy Spirit be with you all. Amen."

6

HELPING HANDS

1879

"Would you like to come with me into the village after you're done, Edith?" Mrs. Cavell poked her head into the front room where her daughter was dusting. She smiled at the pleasing sight of her fourteen-year-old daughter at work. Edith's heavy blond hair was pulled back from her forehead into a long, thick braid. The braid swung about when she walked quickly, which she often did. Sometimes Jack, when he wanted her attention, would pull it none too softly.

"Are you running errands, Mother?"

"Yes, and I would enjoy it if you walked with me. I have to stop by the Benthams' as well, because Mrs. Bentham is poorly."

"All right. I'll be done soon."

Edith stood at the harmonium, carefully wiping off the knickknacks and the sheet music that lay on top. When she was done, she walked over to the mantelpiece and began dusting the Chinese vase and the daguerreotype of Grandmother

Warming. The oval, gilded frame was heavy, and Grandmother's eyes winked at her. She winked back. Although Grandmother Warming had died a few years ago, the family still missed her very much.

"Hey, Edith. Want to play catch?"

Grinning, Edith walked over to the open window and shook out the duster. Lilian and Jack were throwing a ball back and forth on the lawn.

"Not now," she called out. "I'm going to run some errands with Mother."

Jack stuck out his tongue, and she stuck hers out in reply. Then she returned to cleaning the black horsehair chairs. After she had also polished the woodwork, she stood back to survey the room with satisfaction. It always made her feel good to see things neatly done.

"Edith, are you finished yet?" The voice came from the hallway.

"Yes, I'm coming, Mother."

Walking from the vicarage to the village was always a treat. To the east, the purple moors stretched out desolate but with a beauty all their own. When the heather bloomed, Edith always wanted to run and fling herself into its landscape. To the west, there was farmland, hedges bordering the fields.

"I wish I could paint it all, Mother, just the way it is. Do you know," she went on, "that painting is a bit like writing? Father and I were reading Ruskin. Ruskin says that when you paint, you should show the hand of God at work in creation.

Louisa smiled at Edith's enthusiasm. "I'm glad you feel that way," she said. "Your father is a good teacher, isn't he?"

"Yes, he is. You didn't have to be sent away to school, Mother," Edith teased, "because Father, I think, could have taught you as well."

"Ah, but that wouldn't have been proper."

A crow cawed in the field, and Edith sighed with pleasure. "I do so love living here."

"You know, Edith" her mother said as they approached Swardeston, "even if you sketched a different flower each day, I think it would take you many weeks to draw all the different species in our area."

Edith nodded. "Father says there are about two hundred kinds of wildflowers around the common alone."

She stopped to pick some buttercups and playfully held them up to her mother's face. "Your nose is yellow as butter now, Mother. What would Mrs. Bentham say if you came to her door like that?"

Mrs. Cavell grinned and ran a gloved hand across her face. Then she gently swatted Edith. Chatting amiably, they passed the house where Edith had been born. Cows and goats grazed on the common. Cottages laced the main street on both sides—cottages overshadowed by fruit trees. Here and there beehives were set in the small gardens, which contained flowers, shrubs, and vegetable crops. Following her mother onto the pathway of one of the cottages, Edith paused for a moment to pat a kitten.

"Come on, Edith." Mrs. Cavell was already at the steps of the whitewashed cottage with its friendly low-thatched roof. The door opened.

"Hello, Meg."

Meg was the second Mrs. Bentham. Heavy with child she stood in the doorway. "Hello, Mrs. Vicar."

"I've brought you some jam and pasties, Meg. How are you feeling?"

"A bit poorly, but thank you for asking. Please come in."

"Are Maggie, Tom, and Jilly out?"

"Jilly be here, but Maggie's working now at my sister's in Norwich. Might be she's home some Sunday soon though."

"I didn't know . . ." Edith began as they walked in.

"No, she only but left yesterday. Didn't want to go. Cried all the way out of Swardeston, her father said. But it be for the best. My sister's got a small shop and needs someone to help her."

"Oh," Edith said rather lamely and looked at her mother.

"And Tom," Mrs. Bentham went on, "Tom's helping at the bellows by the smithy. Might be he'll get taken on as apprentice if he works hard."

"Where's Jilly?" Mrs. Cavell asked.

"She's bringing her dad some lunch out in the field. Jilly's a good girl and does all the gardening without complaining. Helps with the washing too."

"She's a sweet girl," Mrs. Cavell said, "and I hope she'll help you with the new baby as well when it comes."

"Aye, if this one lives," was the somber reply.

Mrs. Bentham's cotton dress was torn at the armpits, and her bonnet was dirty. Jilly ran in barefoot, carrying a bunch of hedgerow flowers. Held tightly in her thin hands, they were already wilting. She looked at Edith and smiled.

"I saw you on the road. But you didn't see me. I was hiding," she said shyly, "and I picked these for you."

"Thank you, Jilly, that's really kind. Would you like to come over later and I'll read you a story and draw you a picture?"

"We won't bother Miss Edith none," Mrs. Bentham cut in rather sharply.

"Oh, it's no bother at all," Edith said.

Mrs. Cavell gave her daughter a look and slightly shook her head. Edith sighed and looked about the cottage. Unlike its pleasant exterior, the interior looked very poor indeed. Two rusty bedsteads hugged the wall. Yellowed curtains, probably old bed sheets, hung around them in an attempt at privacy. A pair of chairs stood by the rickety table in the center of the room, and a sideboard leaned against the wall. A copper kettle dangled over the hearth and . . .

"Things fine enough for you?"

Mrs. Bentham's rather sharp tone made Edith wince, and she blushed.

"Well, why don't we sit down for our visit," Mrs. Cavell calmly said, as if she had not heard anything. "Jilly, there's a good girl, put the kettle on."

Before she sat down, Mrs. Cavell walked over to Mrs. Bentham and gave her a kiss. Edith marveled at her mother. But then something else happened that made her marvel even more. Mrs. Bentham kissed her mother right back and promptly began to cry.

"Never you mind me, Mrs. Vicar," she blubbered, "the old green monster's in me, and jealousy's a wicked thing, as Vicar always says. You're so kind and all, and never you mind me, and sure but Jilly can come over."

"God is good, eh, Mrs. Bentham," Mrs. Cavell said as she guided her to a chair, "and we try to be his helping hand. Now how about a bit of Bible reading, and I've brought you a bottle of fruit wine as well. Here, Jilly, put it into the sideboard, there's a good girl, and be sure to save it for after the birthing."

"Hide it under the bed then, Jilly," Mrs. Bentham said, "for you know your father . . ."

Later, as Edith and her mother walked home, Mrs. Cavell said, "It would be so good, Edith, so very good if we could have a Sunday school next to the church where children might hear Bible stories as well as learn practical skills—knitting, sewing, reading, writing, ciphering, and mending."

Edith nodded. She knew it had long been her father's and mother's dream to have a Sunday school, a place that would give the village children a chance for some of the education they were missing. The church vestry was too small for such a venture. They would need at least two good-size rooms, where practical skills could be taught to supplement Bible classes. But there was no money.

7

LETTER TO THE BISHOP

Edith and Florence shared a large, canopied bed made of mahogany. It was one of Edith's chores to polish the massive legs from time to time. The bed was covered with a thick, light green quilt, and the girls had often pretended it was a coach when they were little. Jumping up and down with glee on the soft mattress, dressed in flannel nightgowns, they had fled away from robber barons, highwaymen, and dragons. Burying their heads in the eiderdown pillows at the end of their rides, they would giggle and squeal until Frederick came upstairs, threatening them with the rod. But they knew he didn't mean it, for in the end he always sat down on the edge of the bed and tucked them in, more often than not telling a story before he went downstairs again.

The bedroom was an ample, rectangular one. A smaller bed stood across from the big four-poster. That bed belonged to Lilian. The walls had cream-colored wallpaper covered with yellow roses. A large wardrobe stood in an alcove. It held all the girls' clothes. There were a few chairs, a table, a carpet, and a hearth as well, but the fire was rarely lit. There was no need, since the girls generally spent most of their time downstairs in the study with their father, in the kitchen with Mrs. Cooke, or in the drawing room with their mother.

"Did you hear Father and Mother talking at supper time about the need for a Sunday school?" Edith whispered to Florence under the covers. Lilian was already asleep.

"Yes," Florence whispered back. "But they always talk about that."

She yawned and then added, sleepily, "I can't wait to go strawberry picking tomorrow."

"Yes," Edith said, pushing the covers off, as she was getting warm, "but I still wish I could help build a Sunday school, don't you?"

There was no answer. Florence had also fallen asleep.

The moon was almost full and shone brightly through yellow, chintz curtains. A dog barked somewhere in the distance, and Edith smiled. Father and Mother had given her Reddie for her tenth birthday. The puppy was all she had ever hoped for. She had begged for one for a long time. He was four years old now and as beautiful a sheepdog as she had ever seen. The only problem was that Mrs. Cooke insisted Reddie sleep in the stable with the horse. And so he did, because in household matters Mrs. Cooke's word was law.

Edith swung her legs over the edge of the bed and hopped out. Walking over to the window, she bathed in the moonlight. What a still night it was. How wonderfully wide the heavens were, and how incredible it was that God had created them by just speaking. She could say many things, wish for many things, but she did not have the power to speak and make things happen. For example, if she said "Sunday school," well, it just wouldn't be there. Even so, she tested the words softly.

"Sunday school."

But next to the moon, the stars, and the trees, there was only her whisper swaying in a soft evening breeze. Suddenly an inspiration took hold of Edith, and she turned, padding over to the table. After she had lighted a candle, she took some paper out of the table drawer. Then she sat down and dipped the nib of her pen into the inkwell.

"*Honorable Bishop*," she wrote in a firm, clear hand, crossing it out again just as fast. Was a bishop to be addressed as honorable? It didn't sound very friendly. And should she actually write the bishop about the Sunday school? Thoughtfully biting the end of her pen, she stared at the flickering candle.

Perhaps she should write to Sir Hugh Creighton, the local squire. Sir Hugh Creighton only came to church at Christmas and at Easter. A two-timing Christian, Father said, so perhaps he was not the one to whom she should write. But the bishop of Norwich, well, he actually had to be in church every Sunday and he would also be aware of the needs of the poor, as he likely had a lot of them in Norwich, which was a lot bigger than Swardeston.

She began again, on a fresh sheet of paper:

Dear Honorable Bishop, my name is Edith Cavell. I am fourteen years old and live in Swardeston, where my father is the vicar. I think that you must know him. He works very hard and loves all the people here very much. There is a great need here, Honorable Bishop, for a Sunday school so that children might learn Bible lessons as well as some useful occupations such as knitting and sewing and such. But we have no money to build a Sunday school. My father used all his money to build the vicarage, and there is nothing left, not even a farthing. I wonder, Honorable Bishop, if you might have

*some money which you are not using in your cathedral which you
could spare for Swardeston?*

Yours sincerely,
Edith Cavell

Holding up the paper she read it through twice, was quite satisfied, and used the blotter. Then she took an envelope out of the drawer, as well as a penny stamp. Neatly folding the letter, she tucked it into the envelope.

Nearly two weeks passed, and Edith had almost forgotten about her letter to the bishop of Norwich. Then one day, her father came in while she was making jam in the kitchen with her mother, Mrs. Cooke, and Florence. He stood directly behind her as she stirred a mixture of simmering strawberries. Sniffing appreciatively, he began to recite in a singsong voice:

We may live without poetry, music, and art;
We may live without conscience and live without heart;
We may live without friends, we may live without books,
But civilized man cannot live without cooks.

"Oh, Father," said Florence, "did you make that up?"

"No, actually I did not," he replied as he dipped his finger into the jam and licked it. "A man by the name of Meredith wrote that. And the poem isn't totally true of course, because, as you know, we can't live without conscience."

At this point, he waved a white envelope in Edith's face. "So Miss Cavell," he said, his voice becoming rather solemn, "where is your conscience, I would like to know? Because here's a letter for you from the bishop of Norwich himself. And what have you done to deserve that I wonder?"

Edith blushed and wiped her hands on the white apron she was wearing.

"I . . . " she faltered, not at all sure how her father and mother would react to the matter of her having written to the bishop asking for money. "I sort of wrote him a letter."

Everyone was silent, except for Mrs. Cooke, who humphed rather disapprovingly and muttered something about the fact that children should be seen and not heard. Gingerly taking the envelope from her father, Edith walked over to the kitchen table.

"Did you want to read it in private?" her mother asked.

"No . . . no," Edith replied, her fingers hot and sweaty both from stirring the jam and from nerves.

The envelope stuck to her fingers, and a small red stain appeared at the top corner as she fiddled with it. Coming to her aid, her father took the letter back and slit it open with his penknife.

"Thank you, Father," Edith said in a small voice as he handed it back to her.

It was quiet again as Edith took out a thin paper. There was black, bold writing on it. She read out loud.

Dear Miss Cavell:

I was most happy to make your acquaintance, albeit in letter. It is a good thing to be made aware of the need for a Sunday school in Swardeston—a rather urgent need, I take it. Well, this is my proposal to you, young Miss Cavell. If you can raise a sum of money in your

parish toward a Sunday school, well then I shall see if I can help out
with the rest of the funds.

Yours with Christian greetings,
John Thomas Pelham
Bishop of Norwich

Letting out a great sigh, Edith looked up. Her mother avoided her gaze, and her father contemplated the copper pots and pans hanging from the ceiling.

"I didn't know," he said at length, "that you had written the bishop with regard to a Sunday school."

"Yes," she answered softly.

It all seemed so silly now, to have done something without Father. And in some way she understood that this had probably disappointed him. She swallowed away a lump in her throat. Florence came and stood by her, taking hold of her hand. Mrs. Cooke humphed her disapproval again. Her muslin fichu humphed with her, and both Mrs. Cooke and her humph went back to the range to stir the jam. Frederick suddenly turned and faced his daughter.

"And how does young Miss Cavell propose to raise a sum of money?" he asked.

To her relief she saw a small twinkle in his eyes.

"Oh, Father!" she cried, as she ran into his open arms. "Oh, Father! I do have an idea actually. You know I could maybe make cards—greeting cards—and we could sell them! What do you think?"

"It's a little late to ask me," he said, "but it might be something we could ponder."

8

A Slingshot Donation

Edith walked down the road trying to find a secluded spot where she could sketch. Sheep bleated in a nearby field. She set up her easel next to the road and began drawing the hedgerow blossoms. She spent as much time as she could drawing illustrations for greeting cards. The whole family was working hard to meet the bishop's challenge. Over the last year, Father had written hundreds of appeals in his fine penmanship—appeals to friends and neighbors. Mother and she had painted prayer-book markers, and Florence and Lilian had cut out cards. Even Jack had helped by taking bundles of envelopes to William Alfred Towler, the postmaster. And slowly but surely the farthings, the ha'pennies, the pennies, the shillings, and even the pounds had started coming in, monies not only from different cities in England but also from places as far away as India. Presently the savings stood at almost three hundred pounds.

As Edith worked, her thoughts drifted to the bishop and his kindness. Once, when she was about nine years old, she had visited Norwich Cathedral with her father. It had been truly magnificent. Her father had taken her in through the Erpingham Gate and had pointed out the high Norman buttresses as well as the tower and spire. He had also shown her the bishop's palace. Amazed that a minister would live in a palace, she had piped up that surely Mrs. Cooke would not like to dust there. Her father had chuckled and replied that the bishop probably had a dozen Mrs. Cookes to dust for him. They had gone inside the cathedral, and she had peered up at the ceiling decorations. Each marvelous painting was a Bible lesson—creation to the final judgment. With her father's hand in hers, she had been overwhelmed by the size and the grandeur of the Norwich church. She much preferred the simplicity of the Swardeston church, where farmers and laborers took off their hats in the vestry, where the tall west tower with its friendly belfry shook as the sexton rang the bell, and where the yellow-colored glazing of the windows threw gold light onto the dark oak pews.

"We are a small church," she had said matter-of-factly to her father, as they walked down the broad aisle of the cathedral.

"No church is small," he replied, "because people who worship Christ belong to the universal church."

"But we are a little church, and I like that," she persisted.

"What is little?" he shrugged.

A minute later, as they had crossed over into a different wing of the cathedral, he said, "But perhaps someday we'll be able to build a few rooms off to the side where we might have adequate space for a Sunday school. Now that would be wonderful, wouldn't it, Edith?"

Then he had leaned over and whispered, his voice echoing hollowly through the nave, "Between you and me, daughter, I don't think a lot of children are actually taught in this place."

"Are there no children here in Norwich?" she had asked wonderingly.

"Yes," he had gravely nodded, as he contemplated the vaulted lierne roofing on the ceiling. "Yes, there are children everywhere."

Images of the cathedral vanished as Jack's voice called out, "Edith! Edith!" He was running down the road toward her as fast as his legs could carry him. "Edith! I've just found a bird's nest. Come and see!"

"Where?"

"In a hedge—it's one of those birds with a long tail. You know, the one you said hardly ever visits the feeder we put out. Come on, Edie!"

Edith smiled, folded up the easel, and followed Jack, the sketch pad tied around her neck with a ribbon.

"It's a round nest, Edie, covered with moss, and I saw the bird carrying a big piece of moss to it from an apple tree. And d'you know what he did too, Edie?"

"What?"

"He filched some feathers from another bird's nest. I saw him."

Jack kicked stones as they walked, and they passed clumps of pink and white yarrow at the side. Edith's fingers itched to sketch them.

"Come on, Edie! We're almost there!"

Jack's impatience made her laugh, and she began running. Passing him, she stuck out her tongue, but then he bolted ahead of her like a puppy, slingshot visible in his back pocket. Stopping suddenly, he pointed. "Look, there it is."

Edith straightway saw the nest. Shaped like a ball and covered with lichen, it was precariously wedged into a piece of hedge next to the lane.

"You must tell your friends not to rob it, Jack."

Even as she spoke, the long-tailed tit flew past, a feather in its beak. Its coat of black and pink contrasted well with its white apron and head.

"It's just like a little ball of feathers, Jack. Look at it go! Maybe I can sketch it after I watch it for a while."

"I know, Edie. Let's go sit in that oak. Look, there's a low branch."

They had observed the busy little creature only about five minutes when Sir Hugh Creighton, the local squire, came ambling down the lane. Edith took little notice of his appearance, she was so absorbed in watching the bird fly back and forth. Neither did she notice that next to her Jack had quietly extricated the slingshot from his back pocket and was taking careful aim. But she did see a large black top hat suddenly sail over the dusty road and roll to a stop in a pothole. Startled, she looked past the hat, straight into the angry eyes of the squire.

"Please come here, young lady."

Edith jumped down from the branch, picked up her easel, and slowly walked toward the squire. He was a small man, bald as a billiard ball without his hat, and his bushy, white eyebrows were drawn together in exasperation. Jack had disappeared.

"And what am I to make of this assault—of this most unworthy act—of this heinous crime, I say?" He sputtered and spit as he threw out his sentences.

Edith swallowed. She knew that the squire was given to exaggeration and that people laughed at him behind his back because he was so pretentious, both in walk and talk. His green tweed coat, brown knickerbockers, and white woolen stockings only proved the point.

"Well, young lady! Are you going to answer me? What do you say? Are you going to stand there with your tongue in your mouth? What's your explanation?"

Edith moved toward the black hat and picked it up. Dusting it off, she walked back and smiled at him. "I'm sorry, sir. I think your hat is all right."

"Am I correct that I saw a small boy run away? A young lad armed with a weapon of destruction? A brother, I think, who is prone to bad deeds?"

"I . . . I . . . " Edith faltered a bit, but then had enough presence of mind to change the subject. "I was drawing, sir."

She undid the ribbon holding her sketch pad and held it out. He took it and began to leaf through it.

"Mmh. A sheepdog. Good likeness. Very good likeness! Mmh! Looks like my Shep, I think. Yes. Mmh."

"They're drawings for the Sunday school fund, sir."

Much to her surprise, after he gave the sketch book back to her, Sir Hugh pulled out his wallet and presented her with a five-pound note.

"Here. Take it! And mind, watch that young lad! He could have struck me down dead! Could have killed me! Could have blown my brains out!"

With that last statement he put his hat back on and resumed walking down the lane muttering about lumbago. Edith stared after him before picking up her easel. Then she ran back to the house, crumpling the providential five-pound note to a small wad in her excitement.

9
LEAVING HOME

1884

"Edie! Edie, are you awake? Edie, I'm scared!"

A little voice calling through the dark penetrated Edith's dreams. Groggily she swung her legs over the edge of the bed and got up, making her way over to Lilian's bed.

"What's the matter, Lil?"

She sat down on the edge of her sister's bed and snugly tucked the comforter in around the younger girl's shoulders.

"I don't want you to leave, Edie! I want you to stay home!"

"Oh, Lil!" Touched, Edith bent over and kissed her sister's cheek.

"You know that I can't do that. Father and Mother want me to go to school in Peterborough. They want me to learn French."

"But I want you to stay here and speak English."

"But Father and Mother think I would learn many things at this school, and that's why I'm to go and try Laurel Court."

Lilian began to sob, hiccupping words as she cried. "But you won't be able to read to me from *Gulliver's Travels* . . . or *Pilgrim's Progress* anymore . . . when you're far away. And . . . you always play with me and say poems to me . . . and I don't want you to go."

Edith hugged her and whispered, "You know I'll write you letters, and I'll come home at Christmas. And you know what else? I'll let you keep Wendy Warming."

"Wendy?"

"Yes, you can keep Wendy." In the dark, Lilian smiled through her tears. Wendy was very dilapidated, but she was Edith's special doll. It was rare that Edith let Lilian carry her about, let alone play with her. Shrugging off the comforter, she sat up and put her arms about Edith's neck, hugging her back.

"Hey," Florence's sleepy voice came from the other bed, "I thought you were going to give Wendy to me, Edie."

"Well," Edith countered diplomatically, "Lilian might let you share Wendy if you let her sleep in the big bed with you once I'm gone."

The coach for Peterborough passed through Swardeston every fortnight on a Wednesday morning. Rev. Cavell, with something akin to pain, watched Edith standing by her trunk as she scanned the road for its approach. She looked very grown-up in her black stockings and high shoes. When the distant roll of wheels announced the coach's nearness, she turned and called out to her mother, who was standing a few feet behind her, giving last-minute instructions to Mrs. Cooke.

"Mother! Are you quite ready?"

Mrs. Cavell strolled over, calmly pulling on her kidskin gloves. In no apparent hurry, she smiled as if escorting Edith to Miss Gibson's school in Peterborough was something she did every day.

"Good-bye, my dear," Louisa said, offering her cheek to her husband. Then she quietly went to stand next to her daughter. Edith companionably linked arms with her mother. Mrs. Cavell's blond chignon dropped softly below the nape of her neck, even as Edith's thick, blond braid fell sweetly onto a red, paisley shawl.

Rev. Cavell sighed looking at the pair of them. Lilian, Florence, and Jack all clustered around him, subdued by the fact that Edith was truly leaving. Good-byes had already been said in earnest after the early morning family devotions. This was followed by Mrs. Cooke's special breakfast of porridge, toast, sausages, eggs, and fragrant hot tea to wash it all down. She had humphed when Edith had said she was too excited to eat but had unpursed her lips into a rare smile when Edith had jumped up from her chair and hugged her, praising her as she did so.

"No one, dear Mrs. Cooke, makes porridge like you do, and breakfast in Peterborough is likely to be a most unappetizing affair."

The coach, a four-in-hand, seemed antique with its large and formidable iron-shod wheels. Jack fingered them appreciatively before being shooed away by the coachman. Hoisting up the trunk with expertise, the driver opened the door with something of impatience. The four horses in front snorted, eager to journey on, their hooves pawing a road still wet with the night's September dew.

"Good-bye, all." Edith's voice quivered a little as she looked out the window at her sisters, brother, and father.

"Good-bye, Edie."

It took a great many hours to travel to Peterborough. Dereham, Swaffham, Downham Market, and many smaller hamlets were passed. In some of the villages the coachman stopped, watering the horses, allowing his passengers to stretch their legs and to make use of inns. Others he drove through, the coach wheels rattling over the roads. At length Peterborough was within sight.

"Are you nervous, Edith?" her mother asked.

Edith shook her head. She was and she wasn't. There was something in her that wanted to leave home, that wanted to learn what lay beyond the everyday of Swardeston. But there was also something in her that wanted to always stay within the confines of her parents' house. She couldn't explain it but smiled at her mother.

"It was fun, wasn't it, Edith, these last two years? The sketching and the drawing . . . and then the grand day when the cornerstone for the Sunday school was laid . . . " Mrs. Cavell's voice trailed off. Through the window she could see the rapidly approaching city of Peterborough. It was so much larger than Swardeston. Then she continued. "I'm sorry you won't be helping me teach anymore. The children will miss you, and you will miss them, I think."

"Yes, I will miss them very much—all of them. But really, I'll be fine, Mother. And yes, working together was . . . was a wonderful thing. I'll never forget it."

Mrs. Cavell swallowed a lump in her throat. She would miss this daughter, this girl who gave herself so wonderfully well to those around her. She stared out of the coach window, hoping she would not cry and consequently make Edith uncomfortable. She cleared her throat.

"Look, Edith! Up ahead! There's the Peterborough cathedral! We must be close because I know that Miss Gibson's school is directly across from the cathedral."

She was right. Ten minutes later the coach stopped, and the coachman, heaving down Edith's trunk first, opened the door and bowed them out. Then he drove on. They were left standing on a quiet street. Brick houses leaned against other brick houses with no room between them for gardens or lawns. Curtained windows winked down, and large doors exuded respectability. For a moment Mrs. Cavell was taken back to the time when she had been Louisa Warming and had walked through St. Mark's in Islington with her mother. She had been about Edith's age. The thought startled her. Three years later, she had been married. She took Edith's arm and squeezed it.

"Perhaps," she said, "perhaps Miss Gibson will give us some warm tea with scones. I'm rather hungry, aren't you?"

10

MISS GIBSON'S SCHOOL

The dormitory consisted of eight iron beds placed in double rows of four. Each bed had a cabinet alongside it for personal belongings. One side of the cabinet was for books, photographs, and knickknacks, and the other side had hanging space for dresses. One of the first things Edith did was to place a watercolor of Swardeston on one of the shelves, setting it down just so that she could see it when she lay in bed. Then she arranged her books—copies of Wordsworth, Tennyson, and *Pilgrim's Progress*. Mother had given her *Jane Eyre,* and she placed that on the shelf next to her French, English literature, and history class texts. Then, neatly ending the row was her black Bible.

"It will be your best friend throughout life, Edith," her father had said, "dependable, loving, and instructive. Let it be a garland around your neck, daughter. Don't ever be ashamed of it!"

During the first few weeks of school, Edith got acquainted with her classmates at Laurel Court. On the whole they were a friendly, cheerful group of city dwellers who eagerly questioned her about life in a country village. Days slipped into routine. Edith liked routine. Every morning, after a breakfast of toast and porridge, she and about two dozen other students walked across the road to the Peterborough cathedral. Arriving about forty-five minutes before the service, the girls had to sit quietly and read their lessons while they were waiting. Although the weekday services in the cathedral were short, the Sunday services lasted two and a half hours. As the days shortened and winter settled in, it became so damp and cold in the big cathedral that the girls could see their breath when they whispered among themselves. Edith developed chilblains on her hands and wrote home to ask for thick, woolen gloves.

Classes were enjoyable. Edith soon grew to love Miss Gibson, though the woman in no way resembled her mother. Each day, without fail, the teacher wore a plain black, woolen dress, offset with a bit of white piping at the neck. Short and rather squat, she strolled between the rows of students, her speech flavored with a bit of an Irish brogue. Her expansive knowledge on a host of miscellaneous subjects, knowledge that crept in during every class, captivated Edith.

"Does anyone know what caused the bubonic plague?" she asked during history. "No? Well, let's talk about rats and hygiene."

Ignoring the shudders and moans, she proceeded to explain in graphic detail life in the Middle Ages.

"Who can tell me," she said on another occasion during a Bible study lesson, squinting nearsightedly at the students, "where Tyre is and what it exports today? No one? Well, let's get the map."

It was during one of these sidetracking moments that Edith earned the reputation of being just a bit old-fashioned. Miss Gibson, who was waxing lyrical on the general beauty of cathedrals and their significance, touched on Westminster Cathedral.

"A most beautiful edifice," she began, "and have any of you girls ever been so fortunate as to visit there?"

The majority of the girls in class with Edith were debutantes, young girls from middle-class families whose goals extended no further than finding suitable young husbands after graduation. Most usually sat back only listening with half an ear to Miss Gibson's lectures, but on that particular day Alice Morrison, a seventeen-year-old girl from Rochester, spoke up.

"I've been to Westminster, Miss Gibson. Last year my father bought funeral tickets to go to the interment of Charles Darwin. Father said Darwin was a great English patriot and that we should honor him."

Alice shook her brown ringlets, remembering out loud that she had worn a plum-colored pelisse and a bonnet to match. "I wish the class could have seen me that day."

"I understand," Miss Gibson answered a bit shortly, "but pray tell us, Miss Morrison, what you actually witnessed and felt in the cathedral during this funeral."

"Well," Alice responded cheerfully, rather liking the fact that everyone had turned in their seats to look at her, "I saw the Lord Mayor of London, some Parliament members, and some judges. It was fearfully solemn. And then a choir entered singing 'I am the resurrection.' They sang beautifully. And there was, of course," she added as an afterthought, "the coffin.

It was draped in black velvet and covered with white blossoms. It brought tears to my eyes."

"Yes," Miss Gibson said with a small sigh, "and thank you for sharing that with us, Miss Morrison."

It was quiet for a moment.

"It is considered an honor to be buried in Westminster. But our good Queen Victoria did not attend this particular funeral," Miss Gibson remarked, peering over her glasses at the faces in front of her, "and neither did the prime minister, Mr. Gladstone. Now why do you suppose, if Darwin was the patriot Miss Morrison's father said he was, these two eminent people did not attend."

No one answered.

"Come, come, girls!" Miss Gibson's voice was sharp. "Put on your thinking caps. What was Darwin known for?"

Edith coughed a little nervously before she spoke up. It was as if she could hear her father's voice speaking that day she had taken the blackberry pie from the kitchen window sill.

"He, Darwin, that is," she said, and all the girls turned to look at her, "he was not a Christian. And for him to be buried in a church, or . . . well, a cathedral . . . well, that is a mockery, isn't it?"

Miss Gibson considered Edith with interest.

"I'm sure that's not true," Alice smiled smugly as she turned to reply to Edith. "My father said that Mr. Darwin showed Christians how to read the Bible properly. He helped them see that the Bible should not be read . . . uh, word for word. I mean, literally."

"Miss Morrison is right in questioning your accusation, Miss Cavell," Miss Gibson said. "What is your reason for saying that Darwin was not a Christian? Pray enlighten us."

"Well, I don't really think he helped people read the Bible properly. Quite the opposite, really," Edith answered, clearing her throat again before she went on. "Darwin can be quoted as saying: 'I do not believe in the Bible as a divine revelation, and therefore I do not believe in Jesus Christ as the Son of God.' That quote, I believe, is enough reason for saying he was not a Christian . . . and," she added, "for saying that he ought not to have been buried at Westminster."

Alice Morrison looked at Edith disdainfully, before turning the other way. But Miss Gibson smiled.

"Well put, Miss Cavell," she said. "Well put."

The time at school passed quickly. Edith thrived. Tennis became a favorite pastime, and painting continued to absorb many of her free hours. But although Edith was happy and on friendly terms with many of the girls at the school, she did not become the closest friend of anyone in particular. Learning readily, quick to smile and help out, she nevertheless always remained Edith Cavell, the girl from Swardeston. But she did capture a warm spot in Miss Gibson's heart. Teatime was often spent in the matron's apartments, and the two had many lively and enjoyable conversations.

At graduation, Edith stood at the top of the senior class, excelling in conversational French. Afterward she stood at a crossroad. Should she return home to Swardeston, to her parents, and help out in the daily activities of baking, gardening, sewing, and visiting parishioners? Or should she begin to fend for herself at a post as governess? Would she truly fit back into family routine? And there were finances to consider. Father and Mother were not wealthy, and if she could earn . . . Her thoughts jumbled back and forth. They came and went. Edith regularly scanned the papers for teaching posts and, in the end, made up her mind to try life, for a while in any case, as governess.

II

THE GOVERNESS

March 1, 1888

Dear Father, Mother, Florence, Lilian, Jack, Mrs. Cooke, and Reddie:

   First of all, as usual I miss you all dreadfully much. The days go by so quickly it seems I sometimes barely have time to think. About my post here in Dumfries—well, it's as lively a household as my previous post in the vicarage of Steeple Bumpstead. The only trouble is that it's much farther away from all my dear ones. There's no doubt about it, being a governess is a full-time job. The three Mullins children are a handful, especially Daniel, who is seven, but I think of them as being my brother and sisters and truly feel affection for them all. When I am not teaching, we often play outside and run races. (Remember the races we used to run, Flo?) I've also taught them battledore and shuttlecock, which they like very well.

   It's a lavish household here, Mr. Mullins being a wealthy man. There is a drawing room into which our stable could easily fit twice over. The great parlor has a chandelier, which is crystal and from which you, Jack, would very likely love to swing! The furniture is opulent and luxurious, and I am glad not to have been given the task of dusting everything! I miss our front room. It is as cozy and neat as I would ever wish for myself, should I ever marry.

Mrs. Roberts, who is, as they say, the Big Nanny here, rather asserts herself to make me do chores that are really not within the call of my having been hired. She leaves great big stacks of clothing in my room to be mended. I try, I really do, Father, to be humble and to feel Christian charity toward her—because, quite honestly, I do not like the woman. She often tells half-truths, and makes me appear, in the eyes of Mr. and Mrs. Mullins, to be rather lazy or careless. Only last week she broke an expensive vase, and, if Daniel had not seen her do it, would have made me take the blame.

Also, I have been to the theater. Mrs. Mullins had an extra ticket, and she kindly gave it to me and permitted me to accompany her to see Shakespeare's Midsummer Night's Dream. *It was wonderful. Cassie, the upstairs maid, helped me press my Sunday dress, and I thoroughly enjoyed driving with Mrs. Mullins in a coach to Maddermarket Theater. This theater is supposed to be an exact reproduction of theaters during the 1400s. We sat upstairs in a loge, and I could look down below into a large auditorium at scads of people dressed in their finest. There were huge chandeliers lit by gas, and the carpets between the aisles were, I am sure, Persian rugs.*

But with all that, I am ever your country girl who misses the hedges and the heather moors. Write me again soon and tell me if old Reddie still barks at the crows and if he is allowed to sleep in the kitchen now because of his rheumatism. And do please tell me what Jilly Bentham's sweetheart looks like!

Dear Mother, I do miss your tea and scones in the afternoons as well as your sweet face as it smiled at me first thing in the morning and last thing at night. Dear Father, I miss going for walks with you and hearing your gentle and loving voice. And Mrs. Cooke, I do miss your cookies exceedingly much as nowhere I have been does anyone bake as scrumptiously as you do!

Florence or Lilian, do you suppose you might be able to come and visit sometime? I have approached Mrs. Mullins about this, and she said that a cot could be placed alongside my bed in the room adjoining the nursery and that you would be welcome.

May our good Lord keep you all well.

With much affection,
Your Edith

September 1, 1888

Dear Father:

I am in receipt of your last letter and am writing to say that I am utterly astounded by the fact that a distant cousin would be so kind as to leave me a small legacy. You advise me to go abroad and to travel—to have what you call "a Continental holiday." I will have to think on it.

Meanwhile, I have already been on a holiday of sorts. As I wrote you before, the Mullins family traveled to the Isle of Wight this last month. We stayed at a boarding house. It was terribly expensive, I am sure. The Isle is a very crowded place. Restaurants were filled to overflowing, and were it not for the fact that the Mulllins have connections, I dare say we should not have had any accommodations. We went sightseeing. I took the children to fun fairs, mechanical peepshows, and the seaside. Sometimes I felt as if I were at Lowestoft, playing with Eddy and Flo. Remember how we used to help the shrimpers? Have you ever, Father, wished to be a child again with no responsibilities! But enough self-pity and backward glances!

I was given some free time as Big Nanny had been given two extra girls to help her supervise the children. I did not see the Queen, who, as you know, frequents the Isle of Wight regularly. But I did see the Prince of Wales, and I also caught sight of the Princess of Wales. I know you are not interested in this, Father, but I know Mother will be. The dress that the Princess of Wales wore was made of dark blue alpaca, and it had a neck of white embroidered batiste. It was exquisitely beautiful! I know what you will say, Father. You will say that it is the beauty of the inner spirit that clothes a person and that makes that person beautiful. Am I not right? And are you smiling?

Nevertheless, after all the busyness, I was glad to get back to the relative quiet of Dumfries. And now, what to do? Please remember me in your prayers that I might be given wisdom in this regard. (Although I know you always do remember me, dear Father.)

It is late. The candle is fluttering. (Indeed, I don't know if I ever told you that in spite of their wealth, the Mullins have not got the new gas lighting that so many have.)

> With much affection,
> Your Edith

April 1, 1889

Dear Father, Mother, Florence, Lilian, Jack, and Reddie:

You have never before received a letter from a girl with a legacy traveling on the Continent. But here it is. You need not have worried about me at all. I have traveled well and comfortably and am just back from a walking tour that began in Munich. It was beautiful! Let me just tell you about it!

The plains surrounding Munich give way to gently rolling hills— hills that increase in height as you progress toward the great wall that marks the start of the Alps. My companions were all very respectable, and they all mothered and fathered me, as I was the youngest member of the traveling party. We passed lakes and some charming villages. Many churches had spires that looked like onions. You will laugh at me, but it was true, they really looked like onions! We viewed a monastery and climbed Hohenpeissenberg. (Which is Hohenpeissen Mountain. See if you can pronounce that one, Lilian!) During the sixty-mile walk we stayed at small gasthofs, or pensions. They were very clean, and I slept soundly every night. Altogether I had a marvelous time and was filled with a sense of awe that our great God and Father created all these beautiful scenes.

But now I will tell you of an experience that has filled my mind and heart more than any one of the wonders that I have just described. Indeed, you will be surprised when I speak of it.

I came across a hospital—Dr. Wolfenberg's Free Hospital, to be precise—in Bavaria. It is a clinic where patients are treated without having to pay any fee whatsoever. I was told about this place by the hostess in my pension, who has a daughter who was helped there. For some unaccountable reason I took time to visit it.

Dr. Wolfenberg, to whom I was introduced the first day, was most kind and permitted me to watch a number of procedures. On my fourth day there, a man rushed in carrying an unconscious child. It was a little boy. He looked most decidedly like Jack. The father was frantic and ran to an orderly. The orderly immediately told the father to follow him into a larger, adjoining room. Walking behind them at a distance, I was not even sure the child was breathing anymore and feared the worst.

"Was he run over?" an attendant questioned the man.

"No, he has swallowed something, and it has choked him," the father replied, almost weeping.

Within half a minute the whole place came alive. The child was placed on a table. Dr. Wolfenberg slipped off his coat. A Sister was ready with swabs, and a set of instruments was placed on the table next to the child. His small body was slid along the table until the head lolled back over the end and the smooth throat was tight. In a matter of two or three seconds the doctor's knife had cut into the windpipe and a tube was slipped into place. And then I could literally hear the sound of air whistling through the tube into the child's lungs. It was truly amazing, and I shall never forget it. The little boy was then taken into a ward and put into a bed, a warm blanket covering his body. Later the obstruction, a red button, was removed. He lived.

This single incident and the remaining days I spend at Dr. Wolfenberg's hospital moved me to (please don't be shocked) endow the clinic with an *amount of money from the legacy. They had very little in way of surgical instruments and surely could use the money much better than I could spend it. As you always say, Father, "What do we have that is not given to us." And this is why, and you will be happy to hear this, I shall now be coming home sooner than expected. So please, Mother, begin to look out the window, for soon I shall be walking down the road into your open arms.*

May our good Lord keep you all well.

With much affection,
Your loving Edith

12
OFF TO BRUSSELS

1890

"Monsieur and Madame François have four children, and these range in age from three to thirteen years old. They will be left completely in your charge."

Edith stared at Miss Gibson, who had traveled all the way from Peterborough to Swardeston to give her this information—to tell her that a post of governess in Brussels was hers for the asking if she wanted it.

"I have recommended you, my dear, because your French is impeccable, because you are a born teacher, and because I know you love children."

"Is it a good family?" Mrs. Cavell asked with a tinge of anxiety.

She and her husband both sat on the edge of their horse-hair chairs, trying to absorb everything Miss Gibson was saying.

"I assure you," Miss Gibson answered as she smiled at them, "that Monsieur François is one of the most eminent lawyers in Brussels."

"But the family is Roman Catholic," Rev. Cavell objected.

"Yes, that is true. But this will not affect Edith. She will be free to go to the English church. A lot of people at the English embassy go there, and I'm sure she will feel quite at home. They have an Anglican curate—"

"What are the children's ages?" Edith interrupted.

"Marguerite is thirteen, Georges is twelve, Hélène is eight, and little Évelyne is only three."

"That's a handful of children who speak French, my dear," Mrs. Cavell said, nervously twisting the blue silk of her skirt.

"Yes, it is," Miss Gibson agreed, "but you see, Edith would only have to teach the youngest. The others go to school. She would have to accompany them there and back, but aside from that—"

"What about coming home?" Rev. Cavell interjected. "What about holidays?"

"I do believe that the François family has a chateau near the Dutch frontier, and every summer they go there for a while. It is to be assumed that during this time Edith would be free to travel back home to England."

"It is across the water," Mrs. Cavell said with a sigh.

Edith stood up and walked over to her parents. "I have to go somewhere," she said in a cheerful voice, "and it might as well be somewhere that will allow me to improve my French, which is, after all, a school French and not as perfect as Miss Gibson makes it out to be. And don't forget that the post in Belgium would also show me a part of the world I haven't seen yet."

Her father smiled. He stood up as well and took her hand. "You will do well, daughter, to pray on the matter tonight," he said. "It's a good habit."

"I know, Father," she answered and kissed him on his graying beard. "I know."

The next morning both Edith and her father were up early. As if by common consent, they strolled together over the rectory grounds. It was very quiet, and birds were just beginning their songs.

"I've always been pleased," Rev. Cavell said, "that the rectory and the church are just a little removed from the village. There is a peace here and . . . " He let his sentence trail off.

Edith nodded. She understood.

They walked across the cemetery. The yews, eucalyptus, and oaks stood as they always had. Edith imagined a little girl with a yellow poke bonnet playing hide-and-go-seek between the trees. She sighed. It would never come back, that time. And then she saw herself, right behind her mother and in front of her sisters and Jack, walking to church while Bertie Dow rang the bell. She had not really changed. Or had she? Inadvertently her hands moved up to touch her cheeks, and she stopped to look about. The graveyard with its narrow, winding path had borne the feet of hundreds like herself—and in the end their remains all lay here.

"Life is short, Father," she said.

Her father stopped and pointed to a flat, gray stone on their right. *Sarah Cooke,* the stone read in slanted, italicized letters. *Born April 1815. Died January 1889. Until the trumpet sounds.*

"She made good cookies," Edith said with a wry smile, "but she was a bit crotchety at times. I can still see her as she knelt down when we had our early morning family devotions. She always kept an eye on us children, you know, making sure that we had our eyes closed and that we were paying attention. I was very sad to hear of her passing. How is Bertha working out?"

"Oh, fine," Rev. Cavell replied, "but she and your mother have to get used to one another."

"How is Eddy?"

"Your cousin is well. He has a bit of a nervous condition. Says he'll never marry."

"Father?" Edith stopped. She had only half heard what he had replied to her small talk.

Her father turned and looked at her. "What, daughter?"

"Father, I think I will go. You knew that, didn't you, that I would go? Even though I'm drawn by everything that is here, I do feel that God has a place for me in Belgium at this time. Otherwise why would dear Miss Gibson have traveled all the way from Peterborough to tell me about it? Even as I'm walking about here looking at all the things that have surrounded me since I was a little girl, I have a deep conviction that my life is meant to run its course elsewhere."

Rev. Cavell ran a blue-veined hand through his beard. "You must do as your conscience dictates, Edith," he said.

A dog barked in the distance. Edith smiled. "Perhaps the François family will have a pet," she said, "a dog or a cat. I should love that. Even though I am *un peu triste,* a bit melancholy about leaving, I am also very excited."

Her father took her right hand, tucked it under his arm, and went on walking. "Well, I'll enjoy your company as long as possible," he said. "And although we've been parted before, we're never totally parted, are we? Our road is built on the same rock, and it ends in the same city."

Edith squeezed his arm. "I know, Father," she whispered. "I know."

13

The Whole Truth and Nothing But

Edith was captivated from the start by the stately houses on the grand boulevard on which the François family lived. Gray, cream, and white brick made the street seem cheerful even when it rained, which it often did. At first the wide marble staircase, the lofty ceilings, and the high, heavily curtained windows of the François mansion daunted Edith. An early riser, she almost felt lost when she walked about in the morning. She missed the much smaller and more intimate rooms of the vicarage back in Swardeston. But as the months rolled past, she grew more and more used to the François family and felt as if she truly belonged.

Monsieur and Madame François were a gracious couple, and they were obviously very happy that they had been able to secure an English governess. The children warmly welcomed Edith, or Mademoiselle Cavell, as they called her. Several times during the week, she dined with the family in the great dining room at a long table laid with white linen. Flowers always graced the table, and the glasses were crystal.

A maid served, and a valet held Edith's chair when she sat down. It took some getting used to. Other days, she ate with the children in the nursery. There was much less formality there, and the joking and laughing at her sometimes comical French pronunciation soon broke the ice. Even though Edith's French had been considered excellent back in England, she discovered there were many colloquial words that were foreign to her.

During the early spring months of the first year that Edith was in Brussels, Madame François called her up to her sitting room one afternoon.

"Célie is out visiting family, Edith," she said, as she sat at her desk writing notes, "so she will not be able to answer the door for me this afternoon. Please take over this duty for a few hours, and if anyone calls, please tell them that I am out."

"Very well, Madame," Edith answered politely.

She was wearing a lace fichu, a present from Marguerite for her twenty-fifth birthday, over a soft, blue serge gown. Her blonde hair was swept back loosely from her forehead and instead of the braid there was now a chignon. Edith walked out of the sitting room rather quickly, aware that Évelyne would be waking up from her nap shortly and that the older girls were home from school with a cold. But she turned and paused at the door.

"Will Madame be back in time for dinner?"

Madame François looked up, raising her eyebrows at the question. "Back for dinner?" she repeated, a trifle bemused.

"Yes," Edith said, the doorknob in her hand, "because I can advise the cook as well that you—"

She was not able to finish her sentence because Madame began to laugh.

"I'm not really going out, you silly English goose," she said. "I'll be busy here in my room. I have much correspondence to take care of and don't wish to see anyone."

Edith let go of the door handle. She stared at Madame François in a perplexed manner, her brow knitted as if in thought.

"But," she finally managed, "I cannot, you see . . . well, that is to say, I will not say you are out if you will not be out."

Madame François stopped smiling. She put down the pen she had been holding and stood up. "Am I to understand that you will not do as I ask?" she said.

Edith nodded, not trusting herself to speak. Suddenly the large mansion lost its appeal, and the huge hallway just beyond the door seemed an empty place. But her gray eyes met those of Madame François without wavering. Madame François sensed Edith's determination and tried to cajole her out of the problem.

"It is only a *petit mensonge* . . . a white lie. That is not so bad," she said. "It is not *péché* . . . sin."

Edith shook her head. "One should not even tell a small lie, Madame," she answered. "I cannot say this for you."

Madame François shrugged. She was very fond of Edith and had seen that her children were genuinely profiting from her influence, both in manners and knowledge.

"*Bien, bien,*" she said and shrugged again. "If someone comes, just tell them that I am not receiving visitors today."

Edith nodded, and as she was about to leave, Madame François added, "But to tell them this is not as polite as it would be if you would say that I am not home."

Edith did not belabor the point but walked out into the hall, almost bumping into Hélène and Marguerite. With guilty looks, they made as if they had just been passing.

"*Mesdemoiselles!* — Ladies!" Edith's voice was crisp and commanded attention.

Both girls stopped in their tracks and turned to face their governess. "*Oui?*" they answered simultaneously, and Hélène's childish voice squeaked. Marguerite, a lanky fourteen-year-old, giggled, which prompted Hélène to explode with laughter as well.

"You were eavesdropping?"

The giggles became even louder, and Edith shepherded the girls into the nursery. When the door closed behind them, the girls fell silent and looked at the floor.

"I'm waiting for an explanation," Edith said, as she continued to scrutinize them.

"We heard you talking to Maman," Hélène said, "and we heard you ask her if she would be here for dinner and then . . ." She couldn't continue but doubled up with laughter again.

Marguerite continued, poking her small sister in the rib cage. "We heard you asking if Maman would be home for dinner, and that was really *drôle,* really funny, because Maman always asks Célie to say that she is out if she doesn't want to see people. So we waited to see what would happen because . . . well, because we thought it was, you know, amusing."

"I see," Edith answered rather shortly. "So am I to understand that you not only eavesdropped but you also ridiculed me?"

"Ridiculed?" Marguerite repeated. "*Non,* we admired you and wondered what Maman would do. You were wonderful, *magnifique.*"

"Girls, come and sit by me." Edith walked over to the couch and patted the heavy cushions. The girls hurried over and sank down next to her. She put an arm around both of them.

"You know," she said, "it is wrong to tell a lie. Even a little turning of the truth is not the truth. Your maman is a wonderful lady, and I will not say a word about her that is bad. But I want you to know that it is very important to always speak the truth."

"What if," Hélène said, picking at the embroidered daisies on her dress, "what if my friend has an ugly dress? Must I tell her that it is ugly?"

Edith laughed. "No," she said, "of course not, little one. Besides, whether a dress is ugly or not is usually a matter of opinion, not a matter of truth. I mean, you might think it is ugly and she might think it is pretty. Do you understand?"

The little girl nodded.

"Now as to the eavesdropping," Edith went on. "I don't ever want you to stand and listen to someone else's conversation again. It is like stealing, for you are taking what is not yours. Do you understand that also?"

Both the girls nodded.

"And now for the punishment. What do you think your punishment ought to be?"

"Oh, Mademoiselle!" they cried in unison and Marguerite hastened to add, "We are ill. We cannot be punished when we are ill."

"I think," Edith said, "I think you both ought to write an essay explaining why the truth is important in a person's life."

"Oh!" they wailed in unison again.

Edith stood up. "Évelyne is awake, and I'm going to get her. There's some paper and pens on the desk. So get to work, my children, get to work."

14

HONOR AND A LITTLE DOG

1893

"Mademoiselle Cavell! Mademoiselle Cavell!" Marguerite's voice was shrill with excitement as she ran up the staircase.

Edith met her at the door of the nursery, finger on her lips. "Hush, Marguerite!" she said. "You will wake the dead if you make any more noise."

"But, Mademoiselle," Marguerite panted, "I . . . I want to tell you that we are going to the Théâtre Royal de la Monnaie. Father said we will all go Saturday night. Richard Strauss himself is in Brussels and—"

She paused and took a gulp of air before continuing. "Surely in England they have heard of Strauss, Mademoiselle Cavell."

"Yes," Edith said and smiled, "even in England they have heard of Strauss, but I'm not sure that—"

"Oh, but you must come!" Marguerite said, putting her hands around Edith's waist and whirling her about. "Dance with me, my sweet governess!"

Hélène, who was doing math problems at the table, got up and skipped over to take hold of Edith's hands. "Let me dance, too."

Georges, standing at the window looking out at the street, made a derogatory noise. "Silly girls."

But when Évelyne, standing next to him, took hold of his hands, he let himself be pulled into the room, and soon they were all twirling about humming waltz tunes.

"Good enough," Edith finally gasped. "It's time to wash up for dinner. We shall be eating downstairs tonight with your parents."

"Well, Mademoiselle Cavell, has Marguerite told you that we shall be going to La Monnaie Saturday night?"

Edith nodded and smiled at Monsieur François, who sat across from her, his face partly hidden by the flowered centerpiece. A fire roared in the grate behind her, and the reflection from the crystal chandelier threw rivers of light onto the damask tablecloth. The meal proceeded systematically. There were several courses, and at the end of each course, plates were removed and fresh ones given. Three guests had been invited—Dr. Lavalle, his wife, and Madame Evalier, an old family friend. Talk was both political and trivial. The children ate silently and were polite to their elders. Edith was proud of them.

"Perhaps," Marguerite ventured into the conversation of her parents, "perhaps we shall see Monsieur Max, the burgomaster, Saturday night."

"*C'est possible*—it is possible," her father replied. "He is very fond of music and often attends the *théâtre*."

"The Belgian royal family often goes, too," Madame François added. Then, in a questioning voice, she said, "But I think that the English queen, Queen Victoria, does not often go to the *theater,* is that not right, *mon chéri?*"

Monsieur François chortled. "*Non!* She, the English queen, she is a bit of a stay-at-home. She does not go anywhere, and she wears black all the time since her husband died. She is gloomy."

He contorted his face, pulling down his lips and wrinkling his nose in a clownish fashion. The children laughed, and the guests applauded.

"It must be sad," Madame Evalier ventured, "for the English people to have such a queen."

Edith put down her fork. A Teniers landscape hung on the wall opposite her, and she stared at it. She tried to lose herself in the idyllic pastoral scene, but she could not block out Monsieur François's next words.

"Queen Victoria is a prude—a puritan. Her narrow lifestyle is offensive—"

He broke off as Edith pushed back her chair in the middle of his sentence. Hélène, sitting next to her, stopped eating her fruit, and Georges, sitting next to his father, regarded Edith with wonder.

Concerned, Madame Lavalle asked, "Are you not feeling—"

But she got no further. Edith stood up and began to speak in a composed voice, holding onto her linen napkin. The words came from deep within and could not be stopped.

"Monsieur François, I cannot sit here and listen to you degrade and criticize my queen."

After a moment Monsieur François, taken aback, also stood up. By the time he had done so, however, Edith had laid her linen napkin on the seat of her chair, and her small but dignified form had already reached the door. Consequently, he said nothing. Évelyne looked down at her plate, and big tears rolled down her cheeks.

"Come, come, you are almost six years old now, Évelyne," Madame François said. "Papa did not mean to be harsh, did you, *mon chéri?*"

"*Non!*" he blustered, throwing his hands up into the air before sitting down again, adding for good measure, "The English—who can understand them?"

Later that evening, after dinner, all four children knocked on the door of Edith's room. She was relaxing in front of the fireplace, reading her Bible.

"Enter," she said.

They came in shyly, one by one, with Évelyne holding Marguerite's hand.

"We came," Georges began, "to tell you that we like your Queen Victoria. She is very tiny, that is true, but—"

He did not get any further because Hélène jabbed him in his ribs. "Be quiet!" she hissed, and then went on, while she walked up to Edith. "I think that Queen Victoria is *charmant*—lovely. And she has lovely children. And I do not think that she is gloomy, no matter what Papa—"

Now it was Marguerite's turn to jab Hélène. "Do not pay them any mind, Mademoiselle Cavell," she said, "You were *magnifique!* Quite wonderful! You defended the *honneur* of your sovereign. I think you are amazing!"

"Amazing!" Évelyne repeated and then asked, "Do you have any sweets in here today?"

"Just my Bible," Edith smiled.

They sat on the floor at her feet.

"Read to us, Mademoiselle," Hélène begged. "It is so cozy in here. Please read to us, and let us stay for a while before we go to bed."

"I'll read you the last two chapters of the Bible," Edith said as she turned the pages, "the very last. They were written by the apostle John—a very dear friend and apostle of our Lord Jesus Christ. He was exiled, you know. He was sent away to an island because he stood up for the truth."

"What is exiled?" Évelyne asked.

"It means that he was sent away from his country and was not allowed back."

"Oh," the small girl said thoughtfully, as she stared into the flames. "Does that happen sometimes when you tell the truth—that you are sent away?"

"Yes," Edith answered as she ran her fingers through the child's curls, "it does. But that is no reason not to tell the truth. For in the long run all those who tell the truth will come home."

"Come home?" Georges said, creasing his forehead.

"Yes, come home. Listen." And Edith began to read.

"Then I saw a new heaven and a new earth; for the first heaven and the first earth had passed away, and the sea was no more."

"Where had the earth gone, Mademoiselle?" Évelyne asked.

"Shh," Edith said and read on, "And I saw the holy city, new Jerusalem, coming down out of heaven from God . . ."

And they listened.

The next afternoon, as Edith picked the older children up from school, the wind was quite blustery.

"*S'il vous plaît,* Mademoiselle," Évelyne begged, as she walked by her side, "can't we take the tram today? It is so cold!"

"It is good to walk, Évelyne," Edith said as she took hold of the child's hand. "Healthy children should be able to stand the cold and the wind and the rain."

"But what about poor Jacques?" the little girl said, as she pulled the small terrier's leash. "He is cold, too, and he is not a child, is he?"

"The dog is a dog, and he was made to be outside," Edith replied, feeling a trifle like Mrs. Cooke.

Évelyne shivered, and Edith began to walk faster.

"Stretch out your legs," she ordered. "It's good for the circulation. It's healthy."

The children all knew that only on rare occasions would their governess condescend to use the public transport system. And, truth be told, they all thoroughly enjoyed their hikes with Edith into the forests surrounding Brussels, or into the countryside. She had taught them how to paint and draw, how to gather and dry flowers, and how to collect and differentiate a host of insects. Sometimes she offered rewards for the best collections, giving a watercolor or a pen-and-ink drawing that she herself had made as a prize.

"Look, Mademoiselle," Évelyne said, "there are Hélène and Marguerite. They are waiting for us on the steps."

The girls waved and ran toward them.

"Georges is going home with Henri, so we don't have to wait for him," said Marguerite. "Oh, Évelyne, let me hold Jacques' leash," she continued, all in one breath, "and you can carry my books."

"*Non,*" the little girl answered shortly, holding onto the leash tightly.

"*S'il vous plaît,* Évelyne," Marguerite persisted. Digging into her jacket pocket, she dug up a small bonbon. "You can have this if you . . ."

"*Non!*"

Évelyne would not be budged. Her head, with its woolen béret perched saucily on the brown curls, shook decidedly, and she hit Marguerite's hands as she tried to manipulate the leash away from her.

"Girls!" Edith protested, but in the tug of war that ensued, the leash was dropped, and the terrier ran off as fast as his little legs could carry him.

Hélène set off in hot pursuit, Edith and the girls following. Jacques, drunk with liberty, didn't care where his path led, and he barked excitedly as he ran.

It was a busy time of day. A great many pedestrians strolled on the sidewalk. There were cries of admiration. "*Oh, le gentil petit toutou!*—Oh, what a cuddly little dog!" and "*Quel amour de chien!*—Love that dog!" But no one was able to grab the leash.

Eventually Jacques, trying to dodge the many hands and feet reaching for him, jumped off the curb and was promptly hit by a bicycle, which ran over his tail. His shrill yelp brought tears to Évelyne's eyes. A small circle of people quickly gathered. Marguerite, dropping onto her knees, picked up the small dog. Cries of sympathy abounded from the onlookers.

"*Le pauvre chien!*—Poor little dog!"

The man who had been riding the bicycle offered to take the dog to *le vétérinaire*—the veterinarian. Edith, after studying Jacques's tail, the end of which seemed to be turned in a rather odd direction, agreed that *le vétérinaire* was perhaps the best route to go. The crowd voiced approval, and Edith and the girls followed the man through the narrow, sloping streets of the lower town to the veterinary clinic.

The veterinarian, a pleasant man in his thirties, showed no surprise at the compact little group of people entering his small clinic. Jacques tried to wag his broken tail, whimpering rather miserably in the attempt. This brought a fresh chorus of concerned "ohs." The man who had run over Jacques stood in the doorway, hesitant about whether or not he should stay.

Edith walked over to him and said, "We are very grateful that you brought us to the veterinarian, but you may rest easy about leaving. It was not your fault," she assured him. "The dog ran right in front of you."

The man sighed, bowed neatly, and disappeared.

"Will Jacques die?" Évelyne asked in a trembling voice.

"No," the doctor assured her, "I think not. Why don't you tell me what happened?"

Edith tried to explain but could not pronounce the difference between *queue,* tail, and *coeur,* heart.

The doctor listened gravely, his mouth twitching at the corners, and the girls began to smile as well.

At the end of her explanation he said, "The dog must have a *maladie du coeur*—a sickness of the heart. I better put a bandage on his chest, I think." He winked at the girls, and even Évelyne grinned.

Edith blushed, but then she grinned as well.

On the way home, Hélène carried the small patient, and Marguerite walked next to Edith.

"I think *le docteur* liked you," she teased. "Maybe you should go and see him again for a *maladie du coeur*."

Évelyne skipped beside them, teasing right along. "He was a handsome man. Not so handsome as Papa, but quite good-looking, I think. What do you say, Mademoiselle?"

"I say that you all should go to bed early tonight," she answered, putting an arm around both of them. "It's been quite a long day. That's what I say."

15

BAD NEWS FROM HOME

1895

"Oh, Mademoiselle, I do not like my homework," Évelyne said angrily, stamping her small foot as she spoke and almost falling down in the process. "I wish to stay home with you and to have you teach me as you did last year."

Edith hid a smile behind her hand but made her eyes severe. "You must not speak that way. Learning is a privilege."

"I have to write an essay about my country. I have begun but . . ."

"Why not read me what you have written?"

Évelyne sighed, sat down on the couch, and began to read in a childish treble. "Belgium is in Europe, and its capital is Brussels. It is bordered by the North Sea on the northwest, France on the south, Luxembourg on the southeast, Germany on the east, and the Netherlands on the north."

"That is a very good beginning," Edith said. "Go on. Let me hear some more."

"There are no big lakes in Belgium. But there are rivers. Some of these are the Sambre, the Escaut, and the Meuse. These rivers are connected by canals. There are many boats and barges on the rivers and the canals."

"Well," Edith said, "for not liking your homework, you are certainly doing well."

"Do you like my essay?" Évelyne looked up at Edith uncertainly.

"*Oui!*"

Évelyne stared down at her paper. "My teacher is nice, but I like you better."

Edith sat down next to her on the couch and hugged the little girl. "It's all right. It's fine to like your teacher, Évelyne."

"But I like you better, Mademoiselle. I . . . I love you."

"Well, you can love many people at the same time, dear. The more people you love, the bigger your heart. That's good!"

She smiled down at Évelyne's relieved face. "Now read me some more."

"Well, here is some more. You will like this part, too, I think."

Évelyne picked up her paper again and continued reading. "Belgium has lots of food. Some of the foods are French fries, which I like very much, and another food is chocolate. My governess, Edith Cavell, she really likes chocolate, and for her birthday my brother and my sisters and I gave her a box of chocolates. Mademoiselle Cavell also likes the Belgian waffle, and she sometimes eats three for breakfast."

"Wait a moment," Edith said, "You can't put me in an essay as if all I do is eat."

"*Pourquoi?*—Why not?"

"Because I do lots more and—"

Edith didn't get to finish as Célie came running into the nursery.

"Mademoiselle Cavell! There is a special-delivery messenger at the door downstairs. He has a letter for you from England and will not leave it until you have signed for it."

Edith jumped up off the couch.

"A special-delivery letter? There must be something wrong at home then! Otherwise why else would I . . . ?"

Even as she talked she ran past Célie toward the open door and into the hallway. Évelyne flew out behind her, and the essay fell to the floor. Running down the great marble stairs, feet barely touching the steps, Edith reached the front door in a matter of seconds.

"Are you Mademoiselle Cavell?"

The delivery boy was only a teenager. His blue uniform made him appear older than he really was.

"Yes, I am Mademoiselle Cavell."

The boy handed her a form, and she mindlessly signed before taking an envelope from his hands. Turning and almost tripping over Évelyne, she tore open the envelope as she walked back toward the stairs. Pulling out the letter, she began reading. Halfway up the stairs she stopped short.

Évelyne held onto Edith's blue skirt. "Mademoiselle! What does the letter say?"

"It says . . . it says . . . " Edith replied as she scanned the pages, "that my father . . . that my father is very ill."

A few moments later, sitting down in her own room, with Évelyne standing in front of her, she began to shake. The child sat down next to her and hugged her arm.

"Never mind," she said, "never mind. He will be better soon, your papa. I know that he will."

Edith smiled wanly at the little girl. "*Merci*," she managed, "*Merci*, my little girl."

"Read me the letter," Évelyne said.

Slowly, as if in a dream, Edith smoothed the paper on her lap and began to read.

My dearest Edith:

Don't be alarmed to get a letter in this way, but I thought it best that you know as soon as possible that your father is quite ill. Neglecting a cold, he contracted pneumonia while out visiting a parishioner during a rainstorm. The doctor says that his heart is strong, but his fever will not come down. If possible, my dear daughter, please come home, for I do not know what God has in mind.

I do remember so very clearly how your father, from the first moment that he met me, protected me. He was kind when I first lost my own father. He gave my mother and me a comfortable home when we were about to lose our own. He paid for my education out of his own pocket; and he loved me . . . oh, how he loved me . . .

Edith stopped, for she was weeping. Évelyne, who had sat down next to her, laid her arm across Edith's shoulders.

"Never mind," she repeated over and over, "Never mind."

16

A CALLING UNDERSTOOD

Monsieur François and the children brought Edith to the train station. She shook her employer's hand, hugged the children, and boarded.

"Adieu! Adieu!"

Edith pushed herself into the corner of her Pullman compartment even as the train wheels began their clickety-clacking toward the west coast. She prayed. And when she was aboard the ferry to England, it seemed to her that nothing was so important but that she should reach Swardeston to see her father.

Jack met her at the Norwich train station, and from his hug she could sense that things were not well.

"How is he?"

Jack shrugged. "Florence and Lilian are both home from their nurse's training programs. So Father is getting excellent and constant care. But the doctor does not offer much hope, even though the fever has abated. Father can't keep his food down."

"And how are you yourself, Jack?"

He shrugged again. "I've cut classes. I'll stay home until . . ."

He stopped, and they were quiet the rest of the way home.

It gave Edith a sick feeling to see that the bell pull at the vicarage door had been wrapped in cloth. Father had always enjoyed the ringing of the doorbell. She could clearly recall the many times he had said to her, "It's most often a delightful surprise to find out who is standing on the steps. Most often!" Then he had laughed, and she had laughed, and they had both mouthed, "Darcy Smithers." Darcy was a local farmer who, for some reason, had developed the bad habit of showing up at the vicarage after nine o'clock at night, always wishing to discuss some trifling matter that he felt sure was terribly important.

Inside the house, the smell of eucalyptus leaves permeated the air. And Edith thought of the large trees in the graveyard— the trees that stood sentinel over the gravestones, brought in to do duty before their time. She shivered.

"Edie! You're home!"

Florence almost fell down the stairs in her hurry to fling herself into her sister's arms. They held one another for a minute before another pair of arms wrapped themselves around Edith.

"Lilian!" Edith cried, trying to hug both of her sisters at the same time.

Last of all, Mother came down the stairs. She walked slowly and had, Edith saw immediately, aged since the last time she was home. The girls let Edith go, and she met her mother at the bottom of the steps.

"I'm so glad you're here, child," Mrs. Cavell said. "He's been asking for you."

Edith kissed her mother and then, without bothering about her bags, ran up the stairs.

Frederick Cavell, eyes closed, lay on his back in the big bed. His arms, stretched out helplessly on the blankets, were incredibly thin. He appeared so still that Edith found herself watching his chest to see if he was breathing. Florence came and stood behind her.

"He's not able to keep anything down. He's just so weak, Edie," she whispered.

"Perhaps we have to feed him constantly," Edith said. "Maybe with a quill, letting drops of broth fall onto his lips so that he does not have to swallow a big amount. That way he's bound to get some nourishment regardless . . ."

She stopped. Florence was, after all, a nurse in training. But she needn't have worried. Florence put her arm around Edith's waist.

"What a good idea!" she whispered back. "I'll go and tell Bertha . . ."

Edith had more ideas. She filled flour bags with sand and heated these in the oven. When they were warm, Edith carried them up to the bedroom. Taking the heavy blankets off her father, she slipped the sandbags around him. With the weight of the blankets gone, breathing became easier. Clear broth was fed to the ill man from the tip of a feather. Ridiculous as it seemed, it provided him with the nourishment he needed to keep on going. And Edith read to him.

"He can't hear you, Edie," Jack said.

But Edith was unperturbed. "I know he can," she replied and turned the page of her black, worn Bible.

"I think he's out of danger."

The doctor smiled at Mrs. Cavell, whose eyes glistened with glad relief. Two long and critical days had passed since Edith's homecoming.

Edith, who stood next to her mother at the foot of the bed, squeezed her hand. Her father was sleeping—truly sleeping. His chest rose and fell rhythmically even as the gray tendrils of his beard trembled regularly.

Florence and Lilian packed their bags, and Jack took them to the train station. Then he left as well, and there was just Edith and her parents.

Months of rest followed. After breakfast each morning, Edith strolled around the vicarage grounds. Often she walked into Swardeston, ran errands, picked up the mail, and did some visiting. Later in the morning, she would sit at her father's bedside and read to him. Spring turned into summer, and summer turned into fall. One evening, as they sat in the front room, Edith began to read Augustine's *Confessions* aloud to her father. But it was easy to hear that her heart was not in it.

"Behold, the infant in me has long since died, yet I still live," she read, and then she sighed heartily before going on. "No such immature creature has died within you, Lord, for you live forever, and nothing in you has changed from before the foundation of all worlds." She stopped and sighed again.

In front of the hearth, her parents sat on the sofa. Rev. Cavell had a shawl wrapped around his thin shoulders. He regarded Edith affectionately. "What is it, daughter? You're groaning over poor Augustine as if he had the plague. Is there something you want to say to your mother and me?"

Mrs. Cavell laid down her sewing.

Edith put down the book and stared into the flames. "Well, I love being at home with you and have found . . . that is to say, I have come to a decision." She picked up the book only to lay it down again.

"Go on, girl," her mother said. "You're making me nervous."

"Well, I don't like making you nervous." Edith smiled. "So let me get on with it then. Of late I have been reading Florence Nightingale's letters and diaries before going to sleep. She wrote a number of things that really make me think. I have written down some of her thoughts because they are so profound and . . . and, well, as I said, they make me think."

She looked down at her hands.

"Well, get on with it, Edith!" Mrs. Cavell had picked up her sewing again and now punctuated her words by jabbing her needle into the embroidery. Rev. Cavell patted his wife's knee and motioned to her with a finger on his lips. She looked up and was startled to see tears rolling down her daughter's cheeks.

"I am almost thirty years old," Edith whispered, "and I want to do something with my life that would honor God. Can you understand that?"

Once more Rev. Cavell motioned that his wife should not speak.

Edith swallowed, wiped her eyes, and went on. "I have enjoyed being a governess these past years. I . . . that is to say, the infant in me has died, even as Augustine speaks in his book about himself. Yet I am still the child Edith—Edith, a child of God. But at the same time I am almost thirty years old, as I . . . as I already said . . . and thirty is the age at which Christ began his mission. Florence Nightingale must have thought along the same lines because when she was thirty she wrote, 'Now no more childish things, no more vain things, no more love, no more marriage. Now Lord, let me only think of thy will.'"

The clock on the mantel ticked, and the wind rustled the leaves on the trees outside. Edith stood up, and the book fell to the floor. She walked over to her parents and knelt down by them, placing her head on her father's knee. He stroked her hair.

"What is it you want to do, Edith?" he asked.

"I want to go into nursing, Father. I . . . I wrote down something Florence Nightingale said. Listen, I'll read it to you."

She took a piece of paper from her pocket, unfolded it, and began to read. "A hundred struggle and drown in the breakers in the sea. One discovers the new world. But rather, ten times rather, die in the surf, heralding the way to that new world, than stand idly on the shore."

"I understand," her father responded quietly.

"Do you feel called to nursing, Edith?" her mother asked

"Yes, Mother. Yes, I think I do," Edith answered softly. "And I have never felt it so clearly as now after nursing Father these last few months."

"Well, then, child, you must answer that calling."

"I have," Edith replied in a small voice, "I have. You see, back in April I applied to the Fountains Fever Hospital in London, and I've been accepted. I'm to start December 12 as Assistant Nurse Class II."

17

Fountains Fever Hospital

1896

There was no doubt about it, the work for an assistant nurse was difficult and disciplined. It began at six in the morning and did not finish until ten o'clock in the evening. There was no tea time with Mother or pleasant strolls about the grounds with Father. Floors were washed, beds made, slop pails emptied, trays carried around, and instruments washed. The salary was very small. There was just enough money to pay rent on a small attic room near the hospital and to buy food. On some days, Edith ate while standing in the hospital corridor. Other days, she could only snatch a brief moment of rest on a bench on the hospital grounds.

The wards at the Fountains were filled. They were so crowded that there was barely room to walk between the beds. The lowest of the low came here. Drunks, derelicts, and beggars—people picked up off the street because they had collapsed and could go no further. Their desperate poverty did not discourage Edith. She pitied the poor wretches and smiled at them as she walked past, speaking a few encouraging words to this one, adjusting the blankets on that one, and giving a wave to a third. In a matter of weeks, the patients knew her by name and called to her as she passed.

Hospitals were places of last resort. When someone went there, it was reasoned, he was probably at death's door and not likely to come out alive. Diphtheria was common, and the mortality rate was high, especially in children. Scarlet fever and measles were serious illnesses. Children who caught either often developed bronchopneumonia, quickly passing from this life into the next. Edith was not afraid of death. Neither did she shrink from watching a cut being stitched up or from wiping the vomit from a patient's face.

A little girl was admitted one day. Edith offered her a cup of warm milk, according to the custom of the hospital. But the girl did not immediately put her hands around the mug to drink.

"Please, Sister," she said, "how far down may I drink?"

In a flash, Edith saw the Bentham's cottage, the dirt floor, and Jilly's bare feet. "You may drink all the milk in the cup," she said softly, as her arm cradled the child.

The little girl smiled at her—a smile of pure bliss. And Edith smiled back, confirmed in the fact that she had found the role God wanted her to play in life. But she wanted to learn more about medicine than her role as assistant nurse permitted.

In God's providence, one of the surgeons at Fountains considered Edith a caring, compassionate, and able worker.

He sent a letter to Eva Lückes, superintendent of the London Fever Hospital and an old friend of Miss Nightingale. In the letter, the surgeon recommended that Miss Lückes give Edith an interview and consider her as a probationer at her hospital.

The surgeon's request was granted.

"How old are you, Miss Cavell?" The question rang clear from Matron Lückes's lips.

"I am thirty," Edith replied.

Matron nodded. She was pleased with the answer. Most of the young women who applied to be taken on as probationers were very young. Although they had to be twenty-one to apply, many of the applicants were silly and frivolous. Thirty, in Matron's estimation, was a good age—an age in which one knew one's mind.

"What have you been doing these past years?"

"I was a teaching governess, first in England and later in Belgium." Edith kept her hands folded in her lap, determined not to appear anxious. Although Matron made her a bit nervous, she liked the straightforward questions.

"What does your father do?"

"He is a minister in Swardeston."

Matron nodded again. The answer was solid. The church was an emblem of respectability. Besides that, she liked girls from country vicarages because she herself, although not a vicar's daughter, was also from the country.

"And why," looking still more keenly at Edith, "why do you want to take up nursing? Your father is not a doctor nor your mother a nurse."

Edith met her gaze. She did not entirely agree with Miss Lückes's assessment. Surely Father had doctored people's souls all these years, and Mother had nursed countless women through childbirth, as well as caring for people with whooping cough, bronchial fever, and other maladies. She had watched her parents, and she had been taught to act in like manner. But Miss Lückes might think this reasoning rather naive, so she chose her next words carefully.

"I would like," she answered slowly, "God willing, to be of some use to others. I have recently helped nurse my father through a severe illness, and after spending some time at the Fountains Fever Hospital, I am now convinced that I would like to learn more about nursing."

She would have continued, but Matron was not looking at her any more. Her face was bent over a paper on her desk. Edith sighed and unfolded her hands. Then she folded them again.

"Mmh," Matron said. "Mmh. Yes, I see." She did not look up.

"I—" Edith began. But Matron waved her hand, indicating that she be quiet.

The clock on the bookcase ticked. It ticked rather loudly, Edith thought, and tried not to listen. And then it seemed as if the beating of her heart became as loud as the ticking.

"Well," Matron finally said, looking up again and bestowing a smile of singular warmth on the girl facing her, "you will be receiving word from us shortly. Please go down the hall, first room to the right, for your medical examination. And I thank you for coming."

She stood up and reached out her hand. Edith put hers out as well. Matron's clasp was firm.

"Thank you for the interview."

18

THE TRAINING SCHOOL

1896–1897

A few days later, the letter came in a white envelope. Edith carried it about in her pocket all day. It burned against her side and she dared not open it lest she be disappointed. But in the evening, when all her work was done and she was alone, she slit open the flap and read the contents.

You have been accepted . . .

The words danced before her eyes, and she cried. She sobbed out loud. Wiping the tears from her eyes, she smoothed out the paper in front of her and read again.

You have been accepted on probation to be trained at the London Hospital to start work at the Preliminary Training School at No 99 Bow Road on September 3, 1896.

The next morning, Edith handed in her resignation at the Fountains Hospital. A few weeks later, she said good-bye to all her patients and moved into Tredegar House.

The next seven weeks were filled with lectures in anatomy, physiology, bacteriology, and hygiene. Edith also went to classes in bandaging, sickroom cookery, ambulance work, discipline, punctuality, and accurate observation. Her head reeled from all the information that was being crammed into it. Sometimes when she looked at the cracked mirror on the wall of her room and saw the dark rings under her eyes, and when she yawned her way to early morning class, she wondered if indeed this was God's will for her. On the other hand, she hugely enjoyed the knowledge that was being poured into her. At night, by the faint light of a candle, she often reread her notes and memorized passages. Three other girls shared her room, and one in particular was often grumpy about Edith's zeal to study late into the evening.

"Let it go, girl," she would say, "You either know it or you don't. Blow out that miserable candle, and let's get some sleep."

Twenty-five other students began at the same time as Edith. She was one of the oldest in her class. As she had at Miss Gibson's school, Edith—although friendly and helpful—remained a solitary figure and formed no close friendships.

During their intense probation period at Tredegar House, none of the students were allowed anywhere near the London Hospital. Edith barely had time to scribble a few notes to her parents and sometimes guiltily wondered how her father and mother were doing.

Then, at long last, the seven weeks were over. Several of the twenty-five girls in Edith's class had dropped out; others were found unsuitable and asked to withdraw. When Edith's name was called out in the final assembly, she clenched her hands into fists. Although she was satisfied that she had done her best, she was not sure that the teachers would think so. What if she too was asked to withdraw?

"Cavell, Edith."

She stood up, hands now hanging loosely at her side.

"You are to report at London Hospital on December 1 for a trial period of one month, Miss Cavell. Thank you. You may be seated."

Edith slowly sat down. The girl next to her punched her in the ribs and whispered, "Congrats, Edith. I knew you'd make it!"

The girl smiled, and Edith, teary-eyed and wan, smiled back.

At the end of December, Edith was judged a satisfactory probationer. She signed an agreement to serve the London Hospital for four years. For the first two of these four years, she would be a probationer under training, earning a small salary. For the last two years, she would serve as a fully trained nurse earning a few pence more.

March 1897

Dear Father and Mother:

   How are you both? I am well and learning a great deal. And, as usual, I will try to tell you a little about it.

I was stationed in the Isolation Block this past week. This is the diphtheria ward. There are many children on this ward. Their little faces tug at my heart strings, as I am sure they would at yours. Last night, as I was on night duty, there was a screen around one of the beds. When there is a screen, it often means that a patient has died. And so it was in this case. A mother was sitting with a dead, little girl, holding her daughter's doll. The child looked a little like Annie Southam. You know, Farmer Southam's youngest. Blonde hair, a sweet face, and very clean. There are many children who come in here who are not. The mother did not cry. She just sat by the bed and held onto the little girl's doll. The child had been given the doll by the nurses, as she had, the mother told us, never had one. You should have seen her eyes when she received it. All the nurses loved this child—little Sylvie. She never complained and had the dearest dimple in her left cheek.

There is another child, a young boy, in this ward. He is about six beds over from little Sylvie's. His name is Tom, and he is not doing well either. He is on what they call the "dangerous list." Tom's mother and father do not live together and have always managed to visit him during separate hours. But now that he is doing so much worse, they were notified that poor Tom might not make it through the next few days. So last night they were both sitting by him at the same time. The father was sitting on one side of the bed and the mother was on the other. Tom was awake, and it was plain as day that, although he was very ill, he was greatly pleased to see both his "mum" and his "da" sitting there together. I do believe it will help him.

The London is the largest hospital in the city, and at first it seemed very forbidding to me. But I am beginning to know my way around the wards. As yet there is only one operating theater. I have not been in there but will be in due time.

My room is used by me in the daytime and by someone else at night. This is a fine arrangement. Evaline Dickenson, the night sleeper, is not bothered by me, nor I by her. Besides that, when we do see one another we get along famously. She is a dear girl and an excellent probationer. There is, as I have told you before, hardly enough accommodation for all of us in training.

I will give you some idea of what my days are like—when I am not on night duty, that is. I am called at six, have breakfast at six-thirty, and go on duty at seven. At half-past twelve I get half an hour off for lunch. (Yes, Mother, I do eat!) And then I stay on duty until nine in the evening, getting two hours off in between sometime, whenever it suits the needs of the ward. When I am on duty at night, as I am right now, then I begin at nine in the evening. I collect some food on my way to the ward, and I cook it for myself and for the night staff nurse with me. I stay on duty until eight in the morning, after which I have breakfast. I am allowed outside until lunch time in my blue outdoor uniform, but after lunch I am required to go to bed directly. At six o'clock I am called to attend a lecture by Matron Lückes or someone else, but I am very often too sleepy to listen. After the lecture, I go back on duty for the next night shift.

Well, that will give you a bit of an idea what I am all about right now. I do love you both dearly and miss you tremendously. Please pray for your Edith and write back soon again.

May God watch over you both.

With much affection,
Your daughter, Edith

19

EDITH "NIGHTINGALE"

1899–1900

Like a bird in flight, time passed quickly. Before she knew it, the two years of her training at the London Hospital went by, and Edith faced her final examinations in front of the examining board. She passed. And then, on a center platform in the great London Hospital Hall, she, together with her fellow students, recited the Florence Nightingale pledge:

> *I solemnly pledge, before God and in the presence of this assembly, to pass my life in purity and to practice my profession faithfully. I will abstain from whatever is deleterious and mischievous and will not take, or knowingly administer, any harmful drug. I will do all in my power to elevate the standard of my profession and will hold in confidence all personal matters committed to my keeping; and all family affairs coming to my knowledge in the practice of my calling. With loyalty will I endeavor to aid the physician in his work and devote myself to the welfare of those committed to my care.*

All the girls received pins, diplomas, and a navy-blue, silk veil. After the ceremony, things continued as usual. There were more classes and more ward work. Edith poured her heart into her work. She frequently stood and prayed at the bedside of patients, comforting where she could.

By this time, Miss Lückes had become a good friend. Every Tuesday evening, she had open house in her sitting room for any nurse who wished to visit.

On one of those evenings, Edith deliberately sat beside Miss Lückes. "I'd like to ask for your help," she said.

"You're on the obstetrics ward right now, aren't you?"

"Yes, I am." Edith smiled, always amazed that Matron knew exactly where everyone was. Not only that, she also had an uncanny knowledge of who had chipped a bedpan by dropping it, who had been late for lectures, and who had been reprimanded by one of the surgeons.

"How are you liking it?"

"Well, it's both a beautiful and an ugly place," Edith began. "Ugly because most of the mothers who are there are often very ill as a result of malnutrition. But it's beautiful all the same because there is nothing like seeing a baby born—like holding a little infant who is perfectly formed. To rub a child down with oil and wrap him in a little blanket is a bit of heaven, I think."

Matron nodded. She observed Edith keenly and waited. Edith went on.

"A young woman barely out of her teens came in yesterday. She delivered a little girl. The baby could not breathe properly. Something was blocking her trachea. There was no doctor available, so I took a piece of gauze, laid it on the infant's mouth, and sucked. A mucous clot came up, and the child began to breathe as she should."

Edith stopped, remembering how thankful she had felt when the tiny scrap of flesh in her hands had begun to inhale on her own.

With a smile, Eva Lückes said, "It doesn't sound like you need my help. That was quick thinking." And then with a look of curiosity, she asked, "What is your concern?"

"Well, I was so happy," Edith went on slowly, "that I wanted to laugh for joy. The baby's color became normal, her weight was good . . . so I put the child in the mother's arms expecting her to be filled with joy as well."

"But she wasn't?" Matron's voice was dry.

"No," Edith whispered, "she was not happy at all. As a matter of fact, she almost cursed me for saving that baby. I was appalled—really appalled until I stopped to think that the woman very likely had no job, no home . . ." She hesitated, obviously frustrated, and then went on. "I questioned her and found out that her husband had just died of pneumonia and that there was no money . . ."

"And?" Miss Lückes encouraged.

"Well, the favor is this. Could you hold back part of my salary and perhaps employ the mother in the linen room? I have already told her that I would stand as godmother for the child."

Eva Lückes chuckled. "For this once," she agreed, "I will do it, but you are not to get involved in such a manner with any other young mothers, Edith. Or half of London would soon be in our linen room."

Edith grinned. "I know," she said, and again, "I know."

From obstetrics, Edith was moved to the men's surgery ward. It was a difficult ward, but she learned much. One of Edith's patients was John Caldwell, a young man who had been operated on for paralysis of the spine. Often when Edith sat by the side of a patient who was recovering from surgery, she painted. She carried pastels and paper with her. Children loved it when she drew pictures for them while she told stories. John Caldwell drifted in and out of consciousness. The ward supervisor had told her not to leave him alone.

He groaned. Edith bent over him. "Mother?"

"No, I'm . . ."

"Pain," he mouthed, "pain."

Running a cool cloth over his flushed face, she took his hand in hers. He opened his eyes slightly and smiled at her.

Noting a small, well-worn Bible on the night table, she sat down and took the book on her lap. The young man had closed his eyes, but he held onto her left hand as if afraid that she would leave. Opening the Bible to the fortieth chapter of Isaiah, Edith began to read in a soft voice.

"'Lift up your eyes on high, and behold who has created these things, that bringeth out their host by number: He calleth them all by names by the greatness of his might, for that he is strong in power; not one faileth.'"

The young man opened his eyes and tried to talk but could not. She wetted his lips with some water.

"Read more," he whispered.

"'Hast thou not known? Hast thou not heard, that the everlasting God, the Lord, the Creator of the ends of the earth, fainteth not, neither is weary? There is no searching of his understanding.'"

She glanced up and found John's eyes filled with tears. She continued without looking down at her Bible. She had memorized the passage long ago with Father.

"'He giveth power to the faint,' John," she said, "'and to them that have no might he increaseth strength. Even the youths will faint and be weary, and the young men,' like yourself, John, 'shall utterly fall. But they that wait upon the Lord shall renew their strength; they shall mount up with wings as eagles; they shall run, and not be weary; and they shall walk, and not faint.'"

"Not faint," he mouthed, and a tear ran down his cheek.

Edith wiped it, and after a few moments his breathing eased and he slept. She took out her pastels and opened his Bible. On the flyleaf she painted an apple blossom. Then in clear letters she wrote, "Thou wilt keep him in perfect peace, whose mind is stayed on thee: because he trusteth in thee" (Isa. 26:3).

20

THE FLORENCE LADY

1907

"There's Nurse Cavell! There's Nurse Cavell!"

Children came running, and dozens of grimy hands vied to hold Edith's hand as she turned the corner into a street making up one of the poorest districts of Manchester. A smoky, industrial mining center whose houses were blackened with soot and filth, Manchester was a city where more than 57 percent of all the children died before the age of five.

"Come to see me, Mum, 'ave you?"

"Naw, she's coming to see mine, ain't you, Miss?"

A squabble of voices rained about Edith, all wanting her to look and smile and pay attention. Although she did smile, she didn't speak to any of them directly, but neither did she send any away. After a bit of pushing, the children were content to walk beside, behind, and in front of her.

For the past several years, Edith had worked in many different places. She had helped stem a typhoid epidemic in Maidstone. She had been a private nurse for a number of different families. She had served as night superintendent at St. Pancras Infirmary. She had been assistant matron at Shoreditch Infirmary. And now she was living in Manchester, filling in for the sick matron of the Queen's District Home. Often, as she was doing now, she made follow-up visits to patients who had left the care of the home.

At first, the people of the district had mistrusted Edith. But in time they had grown used to seeing her five-foot-three figure at their doors, and as the weeks grew into months they came to love her. She faithfully walked the lanes, alleys, and courts of their lives to check broken bones, change dressings, and show the women how they might cook a little more hygienically.

As twilight fell around Edith and her young admirers, it briefly crossed her mind that all of the children scurrying about her ought to be bathed and tucked into bed—into a big four-poster bed such as she and Florence had shared. But then she shook her head. Such things were impossible. A bird sang overhead, although there were no trees to be seen anywhere. Low, dark clouds hung over the soot-speckled building at which she stopped.

"Eh, Jackie, this is your place. Miss Cavell's goin' to your da then, are you, Miss?"

Edith nodded and began making her way up the stairs of the dingy boarding house. Jackie followed. The rest of the children stayed in the street below. Edith's blue cloak swished against the foul walls. The sour smell of poverty assailed her nostrils: sweat, grime, and cooked cabbage. The wretched tenement building was home to two hundred people. It had a single gutter in front, a drain behind, and one single tap. Every room was occupied by a different family, and often more than one.

"Mum! It's the Florence lady!" Jackie trumpeted Edith's arrival with enthusiasm.

It was a name the people in Manchester had given her—the poor man's Florence Nightingale.

Jackie's mother came to the door with a smile on her face. She was a tiny lady, almost as small as her seven-year-old son.

"Well, you do good to come and see us 'ere," she said, "and please do come in."

"Hello, Nellie. I'm here to change the dressing on Harry's foot," Edith said, as she walked past the woman and put her black case on the wooden table in the center of the room.

A broken window, patched with paper and rags, let in the last light of the day. A man lay on a bed in the corner.

"And how are you, Harry?"

"Da's poorly," Jackie said as Edith stood by the foot of the bed. " 'e tried to get up this morning but couldn't so 'e swore—"

"Hush!" His mother swatted him about the ears.

Edith expertly loosened the bandages and asked Jack to bring her black bag over. Tickled to be of important service, he carried it over with something of a swagger.

"I do so 'ope you stay about a long time," Nellie said softly.

Edith did not reply. Heavy on her heart was a letter from a Dr. Depage in Brussels. It was getting dark, and the woman brought a candle over to light Edith's work as she cleaned the wound. Harry had caught his foot in some factory machinery, but the wound, though infected, was coming along nicely.

"A little while longer, Harry," she said, "and you will be able to walk again. Just be patient."

Harry grimaced.

" 'ard for 'im to be patient, like," Nellie said, "what with us 'avin to eat and all."

"Better out of work for a while, than never to work again," Edith said, and patted Harry on the arm. "You understand."

He nodded and turned his face to the wall.

"Would you sit for a bit?"

Edith was tempted. She was very tired. Nellie's eyes pleaded with her, and for once she acquiesced. After all, it would not be that long and she would probably be gone—gone from here and gone from England. In truth, she was not quite sure . . . not sure at all, that she should be leaving England.

"Are you well?"

Nellie's question startled her. Usually she was the one asking it.

"You look a mite peaked to me."

Edith smiled. For a moment it seemed as if her mother were sitting across from her instead of little Nellie with her stunted back and her thin shoulder blades sticking out like a milkmaid's yoke.

"Yes, I'm well."

"Well, it must be your innards then, because I do think you're frettin'," Nellie observed candidly.

"Well, the truth is," Edith heard herself say, "I think I might be leaving Manchester . . . leaving England."

"Leavin'?" Nellie's eyes grew wide, and she peered at Edith's face past the candlelight.

"I have received a letter, Nellie. A letter from a doctor in Belgium."

"Belgium?" said Jackie, who was sitting at the foot of the bed. "Where's that at?"

"Belgium is across the sea, Jackie," Edith answered.

"Why—" he began, but his mother hushed him and turned to look at Edith, waiting for her to continue.

"Well, this doctor, his name is Dr. Depage, has a dream," Edith went on, warming to her subject and forgetting where she was. "A dream of beginning a training school for nurses in Belgium. In Belgium, you see, they don't have any schools for nurses like they do here in England."

Nellie nodded but kept still.

"They have nuns in Belgium," Edith explained, "but they have not learned how to be nurses."

"They's Catholic in Belgium?"

"Yes, but—"

"You ain't Catholic, though, are you?"

"No," Edith replied, "and I wouldn't become Catholic, of course. The nursing school Dr. Depage wants me to help him begin would be a school independent of the Roman Catholic Church."

"Well, that's a fine thing," Nellie said softly, "to be able to do something so important as all that. Isn't that a fine thing indeed."

"Do you think so?" Edith said, impulsively laying her hand over Nellie's small one. "Thank you for saying that."

"You've been so good to us," Nellie said. "Ain't no 'ouse in the neighborhood but doesn't welcome to see you come. Why it's been like a bit of 'eaven come down."

"I'm not unhappy here," Edith said. "I'm glad to help. But . . . " she paused and gripped Nellie's hand again, "I think that if I were able to train, say, twenty nurses, that would mean that twenty of them would eventually be able to help as I am helping today."

Nellie nodded and smiled. "You 'ave to go then," she said. "That's plain as day, for the more there are of you, the better it will be."

Edith felt a tear slide down her cheek. If there was to be no family of her own, if God did not mean for her to marry—and it did not seem that he did—then these people were her children, and she loved them dearly.

" 'ere now, don't be wettin' me table none," Nellie attempted to joke, but at the same time, she patted Edith's hand furiously.

Edith wiped her cheek and stood up. "I must be going again," she said.

"You light the liddy, Jackie," Harry commanded from the bed. "It's dark out now, and she ain't something we kin afford to lose before it's time fer 'er to be gone."

Jackie grinned and picked up the candle. "Come on, Florence lady," he said, "I'll take you 'ome."

And Edith picked up her bag and followed him out through the door.

21

BACK TO BELGIUM

1907

O Belgique, ô mère chérie,
A toi nos coeurs, à toi nos bras . . .

Without knowing it, Edith hummed the first bars of the Belgian national anthem as she stood on the deck of the steamer that was taking her across the channel to Ostend. The François children had taught her to sing the song with enthusiasm.

"*Le Roi, La Loi, La Liberté!*—For king, for freedom, and for justice!"

How the children had shouted the refrain with patriotism—a patriotism she had to a great extent come to share. Queen Victoria's death in 1902 had brought Edith great sorrow. But the English era in which she had grown up had slipped into the past. Queen Victoria was buried in Westminster, and King Edward, her son, now reigned in her stead. And at some point in the not too distant future, Edith's father and mother would be buried in the Swardeston cemetery under the eucalyptus trees and she . . . She shook her head at her thoughts and scanned the horizon of the Belgian coastline as it rose from the sea. It was by no means the English countryside—a countryside that was embedded in her heart—but she freely admitted to herself as the salt sea spray blew into her face, this side of the English Channel was also very special to her.

The Brussels to which Edith was returning in the fall of 1907 was a different Brussels than the one she had left so many years ago. The first cars were beginning to travel over the boulevards, electric lights were becoming the norm, and many homes now had radios. Also, in contrast to London, Brussels was much cleaner and had more parks.

The coachman drove Edith directly through the city square. With nostalgia she looked at the tall spire overhead with the golden statue of St. Michael standing triumphantly over the dragon. The children had loved to point it out to her.

"There's St. Michael, Mademoiselle. Do you have such a saint in England? One who has killed a dragon?"

The square lay empty just now. August and September were holiday months in Brussels. And in the stillness Edith could imagine the square as it had been in the distant past. Here trade guilds had paraded their banners. Jousting had taken place. Charles V had galloped over the stones on his black stallion. And the cruel Duke of Alva had stridden across the cobblestones, his face aglow, no doubt, with hatred for the Protestant religion. The coach rumbled on. The façades of the houses—gray, white, and cream—brought her back to the first time that she had set foot here. How very young and nervous she had been! Lost in thought, Edith was startled back to the present when the carriage stopped.

"149 Rue de la Culture, Mademoiselle."

She stretched and looked out the window. The driver of the carriage opened the door, took the trunks down, and bowed her out.

"*Merci.*"

When Edith rang the bell of the soon-to-be school, only a portress was on hand to greet her. For a moment the cold hand of fear gripped her heart, but then she braced herself. *If God has called me here, as I believe he has,* Edith reminded herself, *then I must rely on him for help.* She took a deep breath, shook the old woman's hand, and then stepped back into the street. As she looked up at the windows of the four houses that were to shelter both students and patients, the task seemed formidable. She had just two weeks to transform these buildings into a nursing school. Without bothering to unpack her trunks, she went on a tour of inspection, the portress following close behind.

What she found did not entirely displease her. Each residence had its own little garden in the back. Doors had been cut so that the houses could connect at the ground floor and at the basement levels. Edith's office, private sitting room, and bedroom were on the ground floor of the first house. Bedrooms on the second and third floors were reserved for the student nurses. The second house was to have a nurses' sitting and dining room on the first floor, as well as rooms for patients, an operating theater, and a sterilizing room on the second and third floors. The other two houses were to be installed with waiting and consulting rooms for the doctors who worked in the clinic. These additional houses would also provide more bed space for patients. But the only room that was ready and furnished upon Edith's arrival was her own sitting room. Edith sighed, sat down for a cup of tea with the portress, and rolled up her sleeves.

The first girl who applied as student nurse was a Mademoiselle Clara Boehme. She rang the bell a few days after Edith's arrival and was shown into Edith's office by the portress. Edith, wearing a dress of soft dark blue cotton, relieved at the neck by a starched white collar, welcomed Clara.

"Sit down," she said with a gesture toward the chair.

Nervously the young woman, who was in her early twenties, took a seat. Edith well remembered her own interview with Miss Lückes and noted with compassion that Clara's knuckles were clenched white. She smiled at her again and began to ask the same questions that she had been asked many years ago by Eva Lückes. "How old are you?" and "Who are your parents?" and "Why do you want to be a nurse?"

Although thorough and efficient, Edith did her best to make Clara feel at home during the interview and impressed upon her that the vocation of nursing was vitally important. After Clara Boehme, three more young women were interviewed and admitted. The school opened in October 1907 as planned.

The demands of the school left Edith little time for writing letters. But she did manage to write a few back home to England. One of these was to Evaline, the co-worker who had Edith's sleeping quarters during her London Hospital years, a girl with whom she had developed a bond. Hoping for an understanding ear, Edith penned her thoughts.

June 1908

Dear Evaline:

I'm sitting here at my desk taking care of some correspondence that I have, over the last few months, sadly neglected. My only excuse is that it has been beastly busy. Even letters to my father and mother in Swardeston have been somewhat shorter than I would like. And that is why I will endeavor to tell you in some detail how things have been.

Brussels in the fall of 1907 and the winter of 1908 was certainly a far cry from the holiday we spent together on the Continent two years ago. How long ago that now seems! But what fun we had! Do you remember? I dare say you do. But you are married now—a matron in your own right. Is Ireland becoming home to you as, indeed, Belgium is beginning to be to me more and more each day?

Although I began my time here with four probationers, a few more dribble in every three months or so. They are reluctant and eager at the same time. They are full of giggles, compassion, and fear of the unknown. They are young, just as we were. I have to be strict with them, as most have not been taught how to work in an organized manner. So I mix my strictness with love—and I do love them! They have a sitting room with a piano, and after the evening meal I sometimes play for them and we sing. ("Rock of Ages" resounding from a Brussels sitting room seems somewhat strange, but the girls love it!) I also encourage them to come to me for talks. (Remember Miss Lückes?)

As to daytime routine, each girl has five patients in her care. She must wash her charge, feed him breakfast, accompany the doctor on his daily rounds, and carry out the treatment he orders. French is spoken. I can see you laughing and thinking, "I am glad I am not there." But really, I do not find the language difficult. Actually, it gets easier each day. I even catch myself thinking in French. The students will spend the first year entirely in my care here at the school, which is called the École Belge Pour Infirmières Diplomées. Quite a mouthful, I know! The second year they will spend in the surgical clinic. The third year will be devoted to infectious diseases and to midwifery. Then there will be an examination and, if they are successful, the girls will be given diplomas, which will allow them to be employed in private nursing homes or hospitals. Such, in any case, is the plan, God willing.

You would like the nurses' uniforms, Evaline. They are blue, your favorite color, with white aprons and white collars. Their caps are the plain Sister Dora type without strings. (I never did like strings.) Compared with the nuns in their heavy black robes, who care for the majority of hospital and nursing-home patients, my girls look bright and fresh. When the girls first wore these uniforms out of doors, workers in the fields threw clumps of earth at them and yelled, "Ce n'est pas l'époque de carnival!" which means, It's not circus time! The students were a little upset. Actually, they are not too excited about the stiff collar. As a matter of fact, one girl, Helen Judson, was so upset with it that she refused to wear it and made the mistake of coming to observe Dr. Depage (who is the leading surgeon of Belgium) operate in the amphitheater wearing a soft collar. Although Dr. Depage was in the middle of an operation, he immediately noted this poor girl's collar and singled her out. "You are dismissed," he yelled, waving his scalpel about and growing very red in the face. Then he went on operating. Afterward he came to my office, lost his temper again in a most disgraceful manner, and insisted that I get rid of the girl.

"She was improperly dressed," he shouted at me.

"We have not many nurses, Dr. Depage," I responded (calmly, I think, although my heart was pounding), "and it will take some time for these young ladies, used to dressing as they please, to become accustomed to a uniform."

"Then it's about time they began to mind discipline," he barked. (And I really can think of no other verb, Evaline.)

I stood up, because he was rather towering over my desk, and said, "I am afraid I cannot discuss the matter further with you while you use such a tone of voice. Perhaps we can speak when you are more yourself."

Then I walked past him and opened the door. I do confess, I was still a bit of a tremble inside, while simultaneously I also had a strange urge to laugh. He did look so silly and improper himself—his white coat unbuttoned and his stethoscope dangling from his neck. Would you believe that this case went before the members of the school's board and that they voted to keep the girl on? Well, enough said on the subject. But you will get some sort of idea what life is like here.

I have written to Miss Lückes for a matron. Indeed, I write her all the time to ask for competent nurses to aid in teaching and in nursing. (You are not interested are you? Just joking!) Sometimes it gets rather lonely, you see. The Ladies' Committee, composed of society women who have raised money for the school, is sometimes difficult to deal with. Can you imagine that they even object to my serving tea when people come to call! They think it is "beneath my station."

In Belgium, nursing has been looked upon with such low esteem during the last century. This is why it is also difficult to get women to apply. It is said that nursing is no occupation for a lady. I want to raise the esteem in which the Belgian people look at the nurse, and, therefore, the standards I set for my girls are high.

Well, you must think that I am letting off steam. And, dear Evaline, you are right! I hesitate to write to my family about these matters. They would begin to worry about me. Father has not been well lately either. *Florence is quite settled in her job as matron in a nursing home, and Lilian is happy in a little cottage at Henley on the Thames with her Dr. Wainwright. Jack is editor of a paper in Norwich—near enough that he can visit Father and Mother from time to time. I look forward to my weeks off with them later this summer.*

Now for some more informal news. I have two good friends! Male friends! Yes, I do believe I have your full attention now. One is named Jack, and he is a Belgian sheepdog. I picked him up from the gutter where he was foraging for food. He's lovely and devoted to me. Then there's Don—Don, who has brown eyes and a most compelling manner. No, this is not a young man either. Don is also a dog, who just this last week came sniffing at the back door hoping for a hand-out. I have just about, much to the despair of the portress, decided to keep him as well. (Maybe she has a right to despair because the truth is that both Cook and I are softies and feed all the stray cats in the neighborhood too.) Back to the dogs—when I walk to the nearby hospital to assist in surgeries, Jack always goes with me, and I can leave him with the concierge. He is such good company. I also take him along on my rounds in the clinic here, much to the annoyance of Dr. Depage. But Jack is good medicine and often brings smiles to the faces of patients who have much pain. And does not our precious Bible say that laugher is good medicine?

Every now and then a young boy named José comes to the back door to beg for food. He was here the first day I came and helped me carry in my luggage. He was so helpful and so utterly alone that I allowed him to stay and sleep curled up by the kitchen fire. He was gone the next morning but reappeared a few days later. And so he comes and goes. There is also a young girl, Pauline Randall. The chaplain of the English church in Brussels brought her to me. Pauline is the daughter of a traveling showman in the circus. She ran away

*from home, if you can call the circus a home, and the chaplain pleaded
with me to keep the child. What could I say? She is an affectionate girl and helps me out around the office. Although she teases the
students, they all treat her like a little sister. And so we are following
in Christ's steps. Pauline is learning to read the Bible.*

    *Well, my dear friend, do write back and tell me how things are
in Ireland and how your dear one, your husband, is.*

Affectionately in Christ,
Edith

22

A SERVANT'S HEART

The next few years were so hectic that Edith barely had time to think. Between daily lectures for her students, assisting in surgeries, interviewing new probationers, sending out bills, writing articles to promote the school, meeting with wealthy Belgian patrons, and running the institute's household, she was a busy woman. But she took each day one at a time, beginning and ending with prayer to her heavenly Father.

One morning, walking up one of the clinic's many staircases, she was startled to hear pounding. Opening the door where the noise was coming from, she found one of the youngest student nurses, broom in hand, cap askew, jumping about with a panic-stricken look on her face.

"What is it, Chantel?"

"It's a spider, Madame," the young woman replied, "a huge spider. I was trying to kill it, but—"

Edith walked in and took the broom from her hand. "Don't kill it," she said, "but catch it and put it outside."

The student shivered. Edith patted her on the shoulder, gave the broom back, and continued talking.

"A nurse preserves life. She should not destroy life if she can help it. Even a spider has a place in God's creation."

Later that day, when Edith entered her office, Marie Depage, Dr. Depage's wife, was waiting for her. Edith had grown to love Marie, who stood as a buffer between herself and Dr. Depage. As much as he was crusty and crude, his wife was gentle and tactful.

"How are you, Edith?" Marie said, "I just made you some tea exactly the way you like it."

"I'm fine, thank you, and tea sounds wonderful."

Edith gratefully sank down into her chair as Marie put a cup of steaming tea in front of her—not weak tea, the way most Belgians preferred it, but dark liquid steeped to perfection. Don and Jack got up from their places by the window and walked over for a pat. Absently scratching their ears, Edith contemplated her friend.

"What brings you out this afternoon, Marie?"

"Oh, I was just passing and thought to say hello. How are the girls doing?"

"Very well. Much better than at the beginning. Some of the new students coming through are quite bright and determined." Stopping, she laughed and picked up her cup. "Poor girls. Sometimes I think they don't know what hit them. They work hard—nine-hour days for six and a half days a week. And you and I both know that the nine hours often stretches much longer."

She took a sip of her tea, smiling as she did so. "You know, Marie. A new pupil arrived last night while I was out walking the dogs. It appears that courage failed the girl on the doorstep, and she ran away when the portress opened the door. I'm hoping she will feel braver soon and return. Perhaps she believed some of the stories circulating about the school and thinks I am an ogre."

Marie laughed with her. "You? An ogre? Come now, my friend! I know no one who is more gentle or loving than yourself—or more capable. And Antoine thinks so too."

Edith grimaced. "Antoine Depage's mouth does not say what he thinks. But I appreciate your husband very much, Marie. I truly do. I've seen him save too many lives not to be aware that underneath all that gruffness, he really cares for his patients."

"Yes, he does," Marie softly replied.

She stood up and began walking around the room, stopping at the window to look out. Then she turned and grinned. "The queen," she said, "has broken her arm."

"Why do you smile at such news," Edith asked, a little shocked. "That is sad. I have seen the queen on occasion. She is a frail, delicate-looking woman and a busy one with three young children—"

"Edith," Marie interrupted, "she wants a trained nurse from the institute to help her. Think of what her request will do for the status of the school! Think of it, Edith!"

Edith slowly continued to sip her tea. The past few years had been difficult. There had been a lot of falling down and getting up again. There was no denying the fact that when summer came and it was time for her to go home for her annual visit to England, she was always glad of the rest. The administrative duties here taxed her strength and—

Pauline suddenly burst in through the door. "Madame! Madame!"

Edith looked up, slightly irritated. She loved Pauline. The girl was like the child she had never had, but she was so impetuous—never bothering to knock or to think before she spoke.

"Pauline," she said, "I have company. You should—"

"Madame!" Pauline interrupted, "Jacqueline is ill. She has fainted and is lying on the floor of the nurses' sitting room and—"

She got no further. Both Edith and Marie were out of the door and into the hall, running for the basement stairs so that they could get to the connecting door between the first and second houses. They found Jacqueline, one of the recent nurse probationers, sitting on the floor, leaning against a chair. Edith knelt down next to her.

"All right," she said, "It's all right, Jacqueline. I'm here to help you."

Jacqueline, a Dutch girl whose family had immigrated to Belgium, leaned against Edith.

"I'm not . . . " she croaked, "I'm not feeling that well."

"We'll get you to bed then," Edith said and Marie quickly came to her aid. Between them, they managed to get the pale-looking girl upstairs into her own bed.

"Please, Madame," Jacqueline took hold of Edith's hand as she was about to go, "please do not make me leave. I just need . . . some rest. But if you send me away, perhaps I will not be able to come back."

Edith smiled. "Make you leave?" she replied. "I should say not. You are one of the best probationers I've ever had, and I need young women like you. Make you leave! Don't be silly, girl."

Ordering Pauline to sit with Jacqueline, Edith went back to the office with Marie. She sat down at her desk, cupping her chin in her hands.

"Jacqueline is rather sick, you know," she said. "It's not the first time she's collapsed in the last few months. She has a recurring infection and needs a warm, caring environment for a while—one I can't give her here."

"So you will send her away?" Marie asked.

"Well, yes and no," Edith said. "I think I will send her to England to my sister Lilian. Her husband is a good doctor, and they will care for her very well for a few months. Yes, I think I'll arrange that. She can come back when she's better and resume her studies."

"You're a mother hen, Edith."

Edith smiled wryly. "I don't think all the girls would agree. Just yesterday I took away some free time because three students were late for breakfast. It is not that I take pleasure in using these steps," she said as she stood up. "It is just that they must learn to be punctual, to do what is required. We cannot afford to have sloppy students."

"I know, my friend," Marie said, as she put an arm about Edith's waist.

The dogs nuzzled Edith's hands, jealously guarding her, and Marie smiled. Edith laughed out loud suddenly.

"You know that Don and Jack growl whenever the students try to sneak outside for a breath of air. The girls get upset because they have no idea how I always seem to know when they open the door, no matter how quiet they try to be."

Marie grinned back. "Your dogs are smarter than Antoine," she said. "He tries to be aware of everything, but he doesn't always know it when I sneak out. Now," she went on, walking toward the door, "I must collect my little son, Pierre, who has enjoyed playing in your garden once more, and go home."

Don and Jack growled, and Edith walked over to the window. "Oh, I almost forgot," she said. "I'm interviewing a new probationer this afternoon. Her mother is Belgian, and her father is English. They are on the steps. Well, good-bye, my dear friend. Thank you for stopping by."

Shifting her attention to the interview, Edith greeted the father and daughter courteously and welcomed them into her office. Mr. Moore was a middle-aged man with a handlebar moustache. His daughter, Ruth, seemed a subdued girl. She sat on the edge of her chair while keeping a good eye on Don and Jack, who lay next to the desk.

"Ruth, as you know," Mr. Moore began as soon as the introductions were over, "wants to become a nurse."

"Yes," Edith replied, smiling at the girl and addressing her directly, "and you would like to know, I am sure, about the rules and conditions of the school. How old are you, Ruth?"

"Nineteen," the young lady answered.

"And why would you like to become a nurse, Ruth?"

"I would like to help people . . . to be of some use . . . to—"

She was interrupted by her father.

"Ruth is actually too young to know what she really wants. Which is why I am here with her." He stopped pointedly, fingering his handlebar moustache.

"Quite so," Edith said, "quite so. The truth is that it takes a bit of stamina to become a nurse."

He stared at her, and she went on.

"Mr. Moore, Ruth will quickly find out whether or not she is suited for this vocation. My girls have to work very hard, especially during the first three months, to prove that they are strong enough to enter this profession. They have to clean floors, dust, carry food trays up and down the stairs, help dress and feed patients, attend lectures—"

She was interrupted by Mr. Moore. "You have no domestic servants to clean the floors, to dust?"

"No."

It was quiet for a few moments before Edith resumed her speech.

"We try to train nurses for service, Mr. Moore. I think," and she turned her face directly to Ruth, "I think there is a great deal of opportunity to help people, to be of use, as you put it. If indeed, Ruth, you want to serve."

The young woman smiled at her. "I do," she said.

Mr. Moore shifted uneasily in his chair. "You don't really know what you want, Ruth," he said, "or why."

"She will find out, Mr. Moore. And it is good to remember that man considers deeds, but God weighs intentions."

After the Moores had left, Edith sat quietly at her desk, chin in her hand, thanking God for the gift of her own father. How he had encouraged and trained her throughout the years, and how she still missed him. His death, a few years earlier, had not really come as a shock since his health had been frail for a while. But how she looked forward to seeing him again in heaven.

23

RUMORS OF WAR

1912–1914

In 1912, Miss Elisabeth Wilkins joined the school as one of Edith's assistants. A hardy English lady, she responded with eagerness to an advertisement for staff that Edith had placed in the English magazine *Nursing Mirror.* In a very short time, Edith became aware that the sturdy English woman was a first-rate nurse. As the months passed, she also grew to value Elisabeth as a dear and trustworthy friend.

Grace Jemmett also came to live with Edith. A young woman in her early twenties, Grace was the daughter of a friend of Edith's sister, Lilian. During a serious illness, Grace had become addicted to morphine, and Dr. Wainwright, Lilian's husband, thought that a complete change of environment might do her a world of good. During one of Edith's visits back in England, Dr. Wainwright asked if she would take Grace to Brussels with her. Edith agreed, and Grace settled in nicely. The young woman was beautiful and liked to laugh, and Pauline adored her. Edith tried to mother Grace, had her stay in her own room so that she could keep a close eye on her, and spent as much of her limited spare time with her as she could.

By 1914, the school had established a sterling reputation. But the small clinic couldn't provide enough patients to train the new students, who now numbered more than sixty. The board, after much planning, was able to raise the necessary funds to build a new school projected to be finished in 1916.

One day, Elisabeth met Edith on her way out of the office to deal with another in the endless string of demands that kept her on the run.

"You are far too busy, Edith. Listen to me for a minute," Elisabeth said, firmly taking Edith's arm and guiding her back into the office. "Come and sit down for a little while."

Smiling wearily at her assistant, Edith let herself be led back in and sat down. She had to admit that it did feel good. She sighed and took the tea Elisabeth gave her.

"I know that you are leaving for your holidays the day after tomorrow," Elisabeth said, "but I just want to say this to you with regard to the upcoming school year." She frowned with concern. "You must learn to relax a little more, Edith. You're up early, have breakfast with all the girls, and then head right out to assist in whatever operation Dr. Depage or the other doctors are performing. My dear girl, your hair is turning gray at the temples, and you are not yet fifty. Next year, why not sleep a little later and let me take over some of your duties?"

Edith shook her head and was about to put down her cup and get up but Elisabeth determinedly continued.

"You attend all the talks given by the doctors to the nurses. Then, as you eat lunch with the probationers, you cannot sit quietly for even ten minutes or so but must use that time to lecture to them. Now," she waved her arms as Edith began to respond, motioning that she should listen, "I realize that you have a lot of information and learning to pass on, but there is no need to get up and illustrate with diagrams during lunch. Let the girls look at their potatoes and meat for a change."

Edith looked down at her cup, feeling a trifle ashamed. But she did so love to draw diagrams to illustrate her points.

"Then," Elisabeth went on, "you usually interview prospective candidates, and if you don't do that, you walk to the surgical institute or to St-Jean Hospital or to St-Gilles Hospital and make the rounds. If you don't do that, you write articles until supper time, after which you generally have some students in your apartment to speak to on some matter or other. And," she added, "I haven't even spoken about the fact that you run the finances of the school. You send out the bills, track down late payments—"

"Stop it, Elisabeth," Edith said. "You are making me out to be far too hard-working. You yourself just mentioned that my holidays are coming up and I shall be with my mother in Norwich for a good four weeks or so beginning—"

"And that is another thing," Elisabeth interrupted, ignoring Edith's protest. "Actually I don't think you should be going to England at all this year. I know that you bury your nose in school matters all the time, but surely you realize that the political situation in Europe at this time is rather unhealthy. The Kaiser—"

Edith smacked down her cup on the table with a bang. Her smile had vanished. "The Kaiser! You know as well as I do, Elisabeth, that the man is first cousin to our King Edward."

"Well, I don't think that will stop him from declaring war," Elisabeth retorted. "He has challenged British naval supremacy, and the naval race has been going on all the while you interviewed girls and planned for the new clinic to be built. And I am not at all happy about you crossing the channel at this time."

Edith got up, walked over to Elisabeth, and put an arm around her shoulders. "You are a dear friend," she said, "but I think you have a bit of the German phobia that I know a lot of English people have right now. Nothing will happen. France is England's ally, and so is Russia."

"But, Edith, stop to think about it!" Elisabeth protested. "Germany has allies, too. She has Austria-Hungary and Italy. They are all great powers, and they have all taken sides. Besides that, last week the Archduke Francis Ferdinand—"

"Francis Ferdinand?"

Elisabeth sighed and patiently went on to explain. "He was heir to the throne of Austria-Hungary, Edith, and he was assassinated by a Slav fanatic in a little town called Sarajevo, while you were assisting a surgery."

Edith shook her head. "Mother's health has not been the best since Father died. I want to go home. Mother and I will not to go to the sea coast this year but will stay quietly in her home in Norwich. I plan to do some gardening and—"

"Have you heard anything I've said, Edith?"

Edith smiled. "Of course I have. And I know that I leave the school in your very capable and loving hands. I also know that you are very concerned for my safety. And I must tell you that it warms my heart to know that you care about me."

24

A STORM UNLEASHED

1914

"It is a good year for flowers."

Mrs. Cavell spoke from a lawn chair as she watched Edith weed daisies and hollyhocks on her knees.

"Yes, it is rather, isn't it?"

Edith sat down on the grass and smiled affectionately at her mother. Bees hummed about, and the air shimmered with color and life. There was no committee knocking at her door to demand this or that change, no parents to suggest that their daughter was being worked too hard, and no surgery she had to attend. She sighed deeply and pulled at her poke bonnet. The last two weeks had been wonderful.

"Keep your bonnet on, dear. The sun is hot and bright."

Edith smiled indulgently and let her hands slide into her lap.

"Shall I get you some lemonade, Mother?"

Mrs. Cavell nodded. Even though the Swardeston vicarage was now occupied by a young curate and his wife, she felt that Edith's presence here with her in Norwich more than compensated that loss. They reminisced endlessly. She could unfailingly say, "Remember when . . . " and "Do you recall that . . . " And Edith always remembered.

"Here's your lemonade, Mother." Edith handed her mother a glass, brimful and tart, just the way she liked it.

"Thank you, dear."

Just then Mr. Russell, a neighbor, appeared at the fence. His face was pinched and white. "Did you hear," he began, without bothering about the usual pleasantries, "that Germany has declared war on Russia and France?"

For days Edith had been expecting it, had been hoping that it would not happen, and had been praying that God would prevent it. She had known all along that Elisabeth Wilkins had been right in her assessment of the situation. And now, between the flowers and the lemonade, the storm brewing in Europe was sprouting up on her mother's lawn in Norwich—a weed she would not be able to dig out. She put down the trowel she had just picked up again.

"I must leave, Mother." Edith spoke as quietly as the tears that began to course down Mrs. Cavell's cheeks.

The old neighbor, not willing to be caught in a personal confrontation, shuffled back to his home.

"The girls at school will need me. I must go back."

"You can join a field hospital here. They will need nurses in England as well."

By now Edith was weeping too, but she remained adamant in her decision. "No, I feel I must help out in Belgium. I cannot explain it. God dictates my conscience, Mother."

In the end Mrs. Cavell gave up. She kissed her daughter and the very next day waved good-bye.

Although it had been difficult to secure passage across the channel to Ostend, Edith managed it with the help of Eddy and Jack. Both the train station and the ferry dock were a madhouse of activity. Germans were rushing back home to Germany as young men were being mobilized into the army. English families were scurrying back into England from the Continent. Likewise French, Dutch, Belgian, Russian, Italian, and Austrian people were desperate to get back to their countries before the frontiers closed.

The mood on the overcrowded ferry steamer to Ostend was one of apprehension. Passengers scanned the water for dangerous weather as well as for torpedoes. Edith sat quietly on deck, trunks stashed neatly next to her. Her thoughts alternated between the aging and frail mother she had left behind and the chaos and confusion she would, no doubt, encounter on her return to the school.

After a few hours on the ferry, there was the hectic docking at Ostend. Edith had no trouble in getting to the nearby train station and purchasing a ticket for Brussels. She had done it often enough in the past. The mood was tense, and she prayed as she sat in the Pullman compartment.

"Oh, Lord, what will happen to our countries? You know, Father. Indeed, you know, and it is all in your almighty hands."

There was a measure of peace after that. Edith even managed to snooze for a bit before the Brussels station. Securing a carriage, she directed the driver to 149 Rue de la Culture.

"Madame! Oh, Madame! I am so glad you are back!" Jacqueline's words greeted her at the door, and the girl almost choked her in a welcoming hug.

"The German girls are afraid," she confided in a whisper as she helped Edith off with her coat. "Public feeling is running high against them, Madame, and they want to go home."

Edith summoned the German students into her office and calmed them. "You must go about your work," she said, "and I will see what I can do to help you get home."

Her very presence quieted their agitation. Almost ashamed they walked back to their patients.

"I'll go to the American legation first," Edith told Elisabeth Wilkinson a few moments later, "and find out what I can."

Elisabeth stood by the window looking out at the street. "Yesterday, the German ambassador to Belgium delivered Germany's ultimatum," she told Edith. "The last few weeks that you've been gone, there have been repeated assurances by the German government that Belgium's neutrality would be respected. But now they ask that German troops be allowed to pass over Belgian soil to attack France."

"Oh!" Edith's eyes opened wide with shock. She sat down and then promptly stood up again. "I'd better go to the legation right away, then."

At the legation, hundreds of American tourists filled the corridors. It took all of Edith's willpower to push her way through to a desk to get the information she needed for her German nurses.

"A train carrying Germans for repatriation will leave for Esschen on the Dutch frontier tomorrow morning," a harried official told her. "Take your students to station Gare de Nord as quickly as you can so that they will have a better chance of getting on board."

Edith ran back to the school, and, scarcely taking time to catch her breath, spoke to the entire staff. "I leave it up to each of you," she said, "to do what you think is best."

Six of the Dutch nurses and most of Edith's English staff, along with the German students, wanted to return to their own country. They were already packed, so Edith immediately walked the whole group to station Gare de Nord, where they would spend the night. She shook their hands, hugged them, cried, and wished them Godspeed. Then she walked back to the clinic alone. It was raining, and her tears mingled with the raindrops. Would she ever see any of them again?

The next morning, as the last train to run for the Dutch frontier took Edith's girls aboard, the people of Brussels flocked to the street where King Albert and his queen were scheduled to ride on their way to the Parliament house. The sun shone. Belgian flags of black, yellow, and red floated from every rooftop. People hung out of windows and massed on sidewalks; even roofs were black with spectators.

Edith and Elisabeth were also eager to see the royal family and to hear the king's speech. They got up early and left one of the nurses in charge of the clinic in their absence. Then they walked to the Parliament house, pressed their way inside, and managed to secure a standing space in the corner of the crowded building.

Just when Edith was beginning to feel overwhelmed by the pressure of the thousands of people around her and ready to edge her way out of the crowd, there was a cry of "*La Reine!*—the queen!" Soon everyone began to call out, "*Vive la Reine!*—Long live the queen!" From where she stood, Edith could just make out Her Majesty's small figure walking across the platform. She was dressed in white, wearing a hat with great white plumes, and was escorted by gentlemen and several ladies of her court. The royal children followed her: Léopold, the Duke of Brabant and the heir apparent; Charles, the Count of Flanders; and the little Princess Marie José. After they were seated on the platform, all was quiet for a moment until the *huissier*—the beadle—called out in a loud voice: "*Le Roi!*—the king!" Then everyone who was not already standing rose as one. And there was no stopping the tremendous shout, "*Le Roi! Le Roi! Vive le Roi!*"

King Albert, wearing the uniform of a lieutenant-general with his sword at his side, strode in and mounted the rostrum. Taking off his cloak and his gloves, he clicked his heels together and made a smart military bow to the audience. The cheering voices faded, and people sat down again. It gave Edith and Elisabeth a better view. From their corner, they saw the king put on his pince-nez before he began to read from a prepared speech. His voice rang out strong. Edith strained her ears to catch what he said. Missing the first phrases, she did hear the question he posed to his people.

"*Êtes-vous décides inébranlablement à maintenir intact le patrimoine sacré de nos ancêtres*—Are you fully determined to preserve our fathers' sacred inheritance?"

The deputies around the king immediately jumped to their feet and cried "*Oui!*" The speech continued, but it was the last paragraph of the king's speech that moved Edith, and many others, to tears.

"*J'ai foi dans nos destinées. Un pays qui se défend s'impose au respect de tous; ce pays ne périt pas. Dieu sera avec nous dans cette cause juste! Vive la Belgique indépendante!*—I have faith in our destiny. A country that defends its freedom can never die. God will be with us in a just cause. Long live independent Belgium!"

Later that day, officials of the Belgian government handed the German ambassador a refusal to permit German troops to set foot on Belgian soil. In spite of the nation's courageous refusal, the next morning German troops crossed the Belgian frontier near the city of Liège. And England declared war on Germany.

25
INVASION!

One morning after the German invasion, José tapped on Edith's office door. Now a young man, he had become the school's houseboy and jack-of-all-trades. He ran errands, cleaned the fireplace, walked the dogs when Edith could not, and made himself useful in all sorts of things.

"Come in," Edith said without looking up from her paperwork. José poked his head through the door and asked, "Will your countrymen, the English, be here soon?"

Edith looked up and gave him a weary smile. "I am sure they will. Liège is resisting bravely," she said, "and with the English troops on the way, the Germans will soon be on the run."

But Edith's optimistic predictions were wrong. Against all expectations and hopes, Liège fell. News followed fast that the next city, Namur, had been captured. The German troops kept marching on. Horrible tales of burned villages, women and children murdered, drunken soldiers, and looting began to reach Brussels. More than ever the phrase "We wait for England" was on everyone's lips and in everyone's heart.

August 17, 1914

My darling mother:

Just a line, and please let me know at once if you get it, as I am afraid my letters do not arrive. All is quiet at present. We live under martial law, and it is strange to be stopped in the street to have your papers and identity examined.

At church last Sunday the organ was not working so the organist played on a little harmonium. Feelings were tender, and the choir members wept as they sang. The curate prayed, "Give peace in our time, O Lord!" and everyone sighed. He prayed for King George V, and after a moment added Albert, King of the Belgians, and then after another pause went on to say, "and the president of the United States." We were all close to tears. The sermon's theme was "You have tasted the salt of life, and you will not forget its flavor." Indeed, we will not.

If you should hear that the Germans are in Brussels, don't be alarmed. They will only walk through, as it is not a fortified town, and no fighting will take place in it. Besides, we are living under the Red Cross. I should be very glad of some English newspapers as none have reached us since I left England. Two of our nurses arrived back on Tuesday from their homes in southern Belgium, having had a great deal of trouble to get through. My dearest love and Grace's. I will write whenever I can.

God keep you.

Your loving daughter,
Edith

"Madame Cavell! Madame Cavell!" José was out of breath as he ran in the front door, slamming it shut behind him.

Edith came out of her office, admonishing the boy by placing a finger on her lips and pulling him inside her room. "What is it, José?"

"The government . . . It's left Brussels! It's gone to Antwerp! I guess this means that they think the Germans will
soon overrun our city."

Each day, the distant booming of guns grew louder. Even
as José spoke, the windows shook. "At the park, Madame,"
José went on, "a strip of paving has been torn up, and they
are digging a trench. I am going to help."

He turned and was in the hall and out the front door before
Edith could stop him. Elisabeth, just coming down the stairs
from the nurses' quarters, looked questioningly at Edith.

"He's gone to help dig a trench," she said.

"I've already heard from some of the nurses that the Civic
Guard has been called up," Elisabeth said. "They're only a
group of untrained boys and young men—clerks, students,
and such. Alice Peeters saw them early this morning. They
have rifles and a small barricade of barbed wire. From all
accounts, they are very patriotic. But what can they do against
an incoming horde of soldiers?"

For a moment an overwhelming sense of fear filled Edith,
and she had to steady herself against the wall.

"Are you all right?" Elisabeth reached out to her.

"Yes," Edith answered softly, "but I am ashamed to say
that I was terribly afraid for a moment. Yet people have faced
worse times than these. We must not lose heart. We have One,
after all, who is more powerful than a million rifles."

Arm in arm, they walked into Edith's office and looked
out the window. The August sun glittered on the trees, and
a distant sound of thunder rumbled across the sky.

The next day, almost weeping, a totally dispirited José
returned to the school.

"Brussels has been declared an undefended city," he said, "and the guard has withdrawn. Now all the Germans have to do is simply walk in and take over."

As Edith hugged the lanky youth, she looked at Elisabeth over his shoulder.

"It's true," Elisabeth said. "What José says is true. To avoid useless bloodshed, King Albert has ordered citizens not to offer any resistance."

José broke loose of Edith's hug and kicked a chair.

Just then Pauline burst in through the door. "Come on! Everyone is on the roof! You can see the Germans coming! Come on, José!"

He followed her out, and Elisabeth raised her eyebrows in a questioning manner at Edith.

Edith sighed and said, "Very well. Let's go and watch. I suppose one should not miss a moment of such historical significance."

From the roof they could see that the sky glowed a fiery red in the east. Clouds of thick, black smoke billowed toward Brussels. Guns thundered so loudly that every now and then windows in the street shattered. Several of the nurses began to panic, crying uncontrollably.

"Girls . . . girls," Edith soothed, her voice full of her usual, unruffled poise, "remember that even though it seems the enemy has unlocked our gate, it is still God who is in control of the house. Now then, look beyond the smoke, for he who is with us is greater than he who is against us."

Her words and her manner comforted them. They grew quiet and huddled together to watch for a while. After ten minutes or so, Edith went down to write yet another letter. The last, she thought, which might still have a chance of being posted.

August 19, 1914

My dearest mother and my dear ones:

When you open this letter, that which we have feared has happened, and Brussels will have fallen into the hands of the enemy. The Germans are very close here, and it is doubtful that the allied armies can stop them. We are prepared for the worst.

I offered our dear Gracie and the other nurses the choice to go back home. But none wanted to leave me. I appreciate their courage, and I would like you to tell the Jemmetts that I have done my best to send Gracie back to them. She is calm and courageous.

There is £100 deposited in the pension fund, which I have never touched and which belongs to me. I beg you, Mother, to take it with my greatest affection. It will replace the little quarterly allowance that I send you. If I find means to forward you the few jewels I have, will you divide them between Flo and Lil? I would also like you to send Evaline the long golden chain she once gave me.

My most affectionate thoughts are for you, dear Mother, and for you Flo, Lil, Jack and your children, and to Evaline.

God bless you and keep you in his care.

Edith Cavell

Early the next morning, the janitress woke up the entire school by shouting at the top of her voice, "*Les Boches sont là! Les Boches sont là!*—The Germans are here!"

Edith, Elisabeth, Pauline, Gracie, José, and Jacqueline all dressed quickly and walked over to the main street. Although every fiber of their beings resented being overrun by the enemy, the sidewalks were crammed full of Belgians. Pauline hung onto Edith's left arm and Gracie onto the right.

Dressed in gray, the Germans marched down the boulevard with methodical precision, goose stepping in columns of four. Bayonets glinted, drums beat, cymbals clanged, and horses trotted. They were a vast, noisy army. The shrill sound of fifes, the singing of German songs, the grinding of the wheels as the guns were pulled along—all these produced an inexplicable weariness in Edith. Revolvers hung menacingly in leather holsters. Extra boots dangled from knapsacks. Small electric lamps were slung about necks. The letters on the German belts read *Gott mit uns*—God with us. Cavalry, infantry, and artillery went by as well as ammunition wagons, cook stoves with fires burning in them, and pontoons.

After watching for an hour or so, Edith returned to the clinic with her little band. But the troops kept marching through for three days and nights, spouting a gray stream of unwanted men onto Brussels' soil.

26

HIDING IN THE SHADOW OF HIS WINGS

"It is our duty as nurses," Edith said to the group of girls in front of her, "to care for all the wounded. No matter," she added, her eyes probing them, "from what nation they come."

Jacqueline shifted slightly from her spot and grimaced at the floor. She hated the Germans with a passion and did not care who knew it.

"No matter," Edith repeated, looking in her direction, "from what nation they come. The profession of nursing knows no borders! Let us remember the words of our Lord Jesus, 'Love your enemies, do good to those who hate you, bless those who curse you, pray for those who abuse you. To one who strikes you on the cheek, offer the other also, and from one who takes away your goods do not demand them back. And as you wish that others would do to you, do so to them.'"

By the end of August, Brussels had become an isolated city, a city almost totally cut off from the outside world.

Newspapers were censored. Bicycles were banned. Taking photographs outdoors was forbidden, along with flying the Belgian flag or owning carrier pigeons.

"I can't believe that Monsieur Dejeuner can't fly his pigeons anymore," José muttered over his breakfast porridge.

"That's because the soldiers think he might fly secret messages out of Brussels," Pauline said, her mouth full of toast.

"Monsieur Dejeuner hasn't got any secrets. And if he did, his wife would court martial him before the Germans ever got to him," José shot back. Then they both burst out laughing.

Pauline took a drink of her weak tea and then said, "I heard there was a *gouvernante*—a governess—in the Ardennes where the Germans were stationed. One morning an officer took out his gun, pointed it at her, and said, 'I think I would like to shoot someone.' She said to him, 'Then why don't you shoot yourself?'"

José guffawed, as did several of the nurses at the table. Edith let them have their fun for a moment. Then she cleared her throat and began to speak.

"I was sure," she said in a low but distinct voice, "as were others, that the war would be resolved in a matter of a few weeks—months at the most." With all faces turned to her, she continued. "It does not seem that this will be the case. Yesterday evening I was given an English newspaper. The British and the French, my dear girls, have been forced to retreat. So our hope of a speedy end to the war seems to be dashed."

Everyone sat in stunned silence. Then Pauline dropped her knife onto her plate and said, "My hopes are not dashed. I know that . . . I know that the English will . . . " She choked to a stop and began to cry. Awkwardly José put his arm about her. Edith stood up and walked around the table. Freeing herself from José's arm, Pauline pushed her chair back and ran into the shelter of her foster mother's arms.

"Shh," Edith whispered, "shh. Don't be afraid."

Buildings everywhere were being vacated for use as Red Cross hospitals. Belgian ladies who once had turned up their noses at nursing now volunteered. Edith and her small group of nurses helped establish these Red Cross hospitals, inspecting and supervising them all. It was a busy time. Although the remaining English nurses were offered safe conduct to Holland by the Germans, they refused.

Battles raged everywhere. Villages were burned and looted. Slowly but steadily, refugees began to file into Brussels: children with terror reflecting from their eyes trotted past in their sabots, widowed mothers stooped as they carried wailing infants, and bitter men pulled dog carts filled with household goods.

On the eastern front, it seemed that Germany was gaining momentum. Russia was not retaliating well to the disciplined forces of the Uhlans. German U-boats had sunk several of Britain's ships. But on the western front, matters settled down. The advance of the Germans was halted at the Marne. A stalemate had been achieved.

In October, Antwerp fell, and the Belgian government was forced to retreat. Baron von Bissing, an old German man, was appointed as governor general. One of the many rules that he implemented was that male civilian patients, when discharged from the hospital, had to report to the German military police. Everyone knew this order meant sure deportation to a prison camp in Germany.

When Edith heard this, she called a special meeting of her nurses.

"As I have often said to you before, we are called to give life and not take it," she reminded them. "We have before us today a problem. When we discharge young men from the hospital, are we to direct them to the police headquarters, as we have been told by the authorities?"

Her nurses looked at her nervously, unsure of what her advice would be. Everyone in the group was acutely aware of Edith's regard for the absolute truth.

"When a patient is ready to leave," she went on calmly, "you will indeed instruct him how to get to the nearest police headquarters."

Jacqueline balled her fists. As if she would! How could Madame Cavell say such a thing! But Edith was not finished.

"You will also, however," she went on, a slight smile curving her mouth, "point out to him that if he takes another route, he will arrive at an address where people will hide him until some way can be found to smuggle him out of Brussels. There are, you see, a host of friendly Belgian citizens willing to have visitors."

Summer turned into a rainy fall. Fog obliterated sight, and it was chilly out. Refugees, like stray dogs and cats, roamed the streets of Brussels. German officers strutted about enforcing silly rules. Two little boys who shouted *Vive le Roi!* were arrested and thrown in jail. Another little boy was taken into custody for mimicking the goose steps of a squadron of soldiers. As conditions worsened, soup kitchens were established. People lined up in the rain, shivering in shawls and old coats, each carrying some sort of container and holding a numbered card issued by his or her district. The soup and bread came from America.

Early one evening in November, Jack growled. Hidden behind the curtain of her window, Edith could make out the shadowy figure of a man at the door. It was after curfew, and she decided that whoever would risk arrest to visit at this time must have a good reason. Not waiting for the portress, she took Jack by the collar, went out into the hall, and opened the door.

"Madame Cavell?"

She nodded, and the man thrust a note into her free hand. She immediately recognized the handwriting on the note as that of Marie Depage.

"Come in, sir." She stood aside, let him enter, and then quickly ushered him into her office.

"My name is Hermann Capiau, Madame," he said, "and I would beg a few moments of your time."

Judging him to be a gentleman, Edith asked him to sit down. She sat down as well and read Marie's note.

Dear Edith:

Listen to Monsieur Capiau. Then act according to your own judgment.

Marie

Taking a second look at her visitor, Edith relaxed. He seemed an honest fellow who was not afraid to return her gaze without blinking.

"What brings you here, Monsieur Capiau?"

"I have been told that you are a good woman, Madame, and I will come straight to the point. In my care presently there are two British soldiers. They were separated from their unit during the battle of Mons and are in urgent need of a place to stay."

Edith looked down at the floor. Around her she heard the sounds of the clinic settling down for the night. She smoothed the letter lying in front of her on the desk.

"Colonel Bodger, I must tell you," Monsieur Capiau went on, "has an injury in his foot, and Sergeant Meachin also has a slight wound from a bullet that grazed his face."

At this moment, Elisabeth Wilkins knocked at the office door before she poked her head around the corner. "Would you like some tea, Edith?" she asked, "for yourself and for . . . ?"

"No, thank you, Elisabeth," Edith answered as she stood up. "That won't be necessary, as this gentleman is just leaving."

Hermann Capiau stood up, his face clouded with disappointment. But to his relief, Edith added, "Please tell one of the girls to make up two beds. We have some wounded men coming in."

Elisabeth nodded and disappeared.

For about two weeks after Monsieur Capiau brought the British soldiers to Edith, everything went well. Then one day in the hall where José was sweeping as if his life depended on it, he urgently whispered, "Madame," as Edith was passing by.

Edith stopped and looked at the boy. He was fast becoming a man.

"What is it, José?"

"I've heard that the Germans are going to search the school in a few days. I think that the Englishmen—"

"Shh." Edith put a finger on her lips and shook her head. There were a number of wounded Germans in her wards, and they all had ears. She and her staff could not claim ignorance of the risk they were taking, because notices had been posted throughout Brussels stating that anyone who hid fugitives would be severely punished.

Standing quietly, Edith thought for a moment. She knew, through Monsieur Capiau, the name and address of a man who was willing to guide fugitives to freedom.

"Prepare a lunch bag with ten slices of bread for each of the men, and have it ready for early tomorrow morning. Do you understand, José?"

He nodded, eyes shining, and went on sweeping.

Edith went looking for Elisabeth and found her in the laundry room counting towels.

"Elisabeth, can you waken me tomorrow morning at four? I shall be leaving together with our . . . our guests, if you understand."

Elisabeth nodded without saying a word.

Early the next morning Edith, dressed in a blue cloak and black hat, left the school. Two men dressed in workman's clothes followed her at a little distance.

Three hours later, Edith reappeared and breakfasted with the nurses.

27

THE UNDERGROUND

"*Schwester*—Sister," said the German soldier as he eyed Edith from the bed, "you are very good and kind. I was afraid at first."

"Why?" Edith asked.

He grinned at her, obviously embarrassed. His comrade, the soldier in the next bed, answered for him. "He thought that all Belgian women cut out the eyes of the wounded. That's the story going around in German troops about the hospitals here."

"Why would you think that?" Edith said, astounded. "Who—"

"Before we left home," the second man interrupted, "there were articles in our newspaper, you see. They said that Belgian women threw sick Germans out of windows."

A smile twitched at the corners of Edith's mouth. She estimated that her patient weighed approximately two hundred pounds. Not exactly an easy toss out of the window of 149 Rue de la Culture.

"The article also said that we would be given cigarettes containing gun powder," he told her. "And that nurses would pour petrol over our wounds and—"

"Well," Edith cut in, "I'm glad you've found out this is not true."

Both the men smiled at her.

"Madame!" the portress respectfully called out to Edith from the hallway as she stood by the bedside of the soldiers.

Edith nodded at the men, turned around, and walked out. "Yes?"

"There's a gentleman to see you, Madame. I put him in your office. He says he's a prince of some sort."

"Very well. I'll be down shortly."

It was evening, and Edith had misgivings as she walked down the stairs to her office. Monsieur Capiau had told her that she might be contacted again, and she had, it was true, indicated that she would be quite willing to help. But it had only been a few days since Colonel Bodgers and Sergeant Meachin had left. And there was a certain attractiveness about not having to hide anything. She steeled herself when she opened the door.

A man of medium height, with dark hair and a black, bushy moustache, bowed to her. Heavily lidded eyes studied her keenly as he straightened. "*Bonsoir,* Madame."

"*Bonsoir,* Monsieur . . . ?"

"—de Cröy, Prince Reginald de Cröy." He took her proffered hand, kissed it, and quietly continued to observe her.

Saying nothing, Edith took her place at her desk and motioned that he might sit down as well. She noted with amusement that he wore a blue bow tie with white dots, something she did not associate with princely attire.

"My sister and I," he began, "live close to the Mormal Forest. A great many English soldiers are stranded there, left behind in the wake of battle. Some are wounded and have been brought to the chateau in which we live. We hide them and nurse them. There are also other people who help—peasants, priests, miners—people who are patriotic, people such as yourself, Madame."

"Mmh," was all Edith would say until she heard more.

"We desperately need safe houses to which we can bring these men on their way out of Belgium, as they travel toward Holland and from there to France or England. We have heard that you hid some men in the hospital . . . and that, indeed, you might be willing to do so again."

He stopped, stroked his moustache, and regarded her intently.

Edith stared at him, and far down the corridors of the past she heard her father's voice:

It is an honor, a great honor to belong to Christ. But with belonging to him comes a great deal of responsibility. If you belong to Christ, you ought to be a refreshment to others . . .

She cleared her throat before she spoke. "I would be honored to help."

He smiled broadly. "*Tres bon*—very good. We, that is, my sister and I, have devised a means of providing men with forged identity papers. Marie, my sister, she is a good photographer and has managed to keep an old camera hidden from the Germans. She takes pictures of the soldiers, and I pick up identification forms from someone we trust at the Bureau de la Population. We staple the photographs onto the forms and insert Belgian names. Then I take them back to the bureau, and that same trusted employee stamps the forms 'Commune de St. Jean Hainaut.' "

He stopped for a moment and grinned at Edith. "There really is no *commune*—no parish—by that name. But no one has bothered to find this out. In this way the men have some measure of safety as they travel to you in Brussels or to other places."

"There is just you and your sister?"

"No, there are others. Mademoiselle Louise Thuliez scours the countryside looking for Allied soldiers. She is a teacher, and perhaps you will meet her at some point in time. Monsieur Capiau you have met. There are more, but you need not concern yourself about them. As a matter of fact, the less you know the better."

"How shall I know," Edith asked, "whether or not the people coming here are your refugees or not?"

"Good question," he replied. "Any ideas?"

"Well," she offered after a few moments of thought, "your name is Cröy and backwards that will read 'yorc.' Perhaps that would be a good code name."

The mouth above the blue polka-dot tie curved into a grin. "Agreed. So if you doubt the honesty of a messenger and if you are not shown a paper with the word 'yorc' on it, you can be sure that this person does not come from us. Also, before I go I would like to give you more details about guides who are available to take the men from Brussels to the Dutch frontier."

28

A Way of Escape

1914–1915

Breakfast was generally served at an early hour in the school—too early, some of the nurses said.

"It is actually seven o'clock, you know," José said at six o'clock one morning, as he bit into a thin piece of toast.

Puzzled, everyone stared at him, and he went on.

"The Germans changed our time yesterday. We are now on German time and no longer on Belgian time. All the public clocks have been put ahead."

"Well, I'm not going to pay the slightest bit of attention," Gracie said, glancing at her wrist watch. "That's just plain silly."

"Well, maybe," Pauline added hopefully, "we should get up later."

She eyed Edith, but Edith was looking at Cook in the doorway.

"Excuse me, Madame," the cook said, "there is someone to see you in the kitchen."

Edith got up, wiped her mouth on a napkin, and left the dining room quietly after glancing at Elisabeth Wilkins.

Elisabeth nodded to her, indicating that she would supervise while Edith was gone.

Louise Thuliez, one of the resistance workers Edith had come to know, was waiting in the kitchen. She had come in through the back entrance. Brown hair hidden under a kerchief, the young woman was obviously relieved when Edith walked in. Ushering her through the hall toward her own office, Edith could feel the woman's tenseness.

As soon as the door closed behind them, Louise spoke. There was urgency in her tone. "I have two men waiting to come to the clinic."

Edith nodded. "Fine. Direct them here. I'll see to them."

Louise nodded, brusquely put out her hand, which Edith shook, and disappeared.

Left alone in her small office, Edith passed her right hand over her forehead in a gesture of weariness. Running a hospital in peacetime was not easy, but running it in wartime, with mounting bills for food and medicines that would never be paid by the patients, was next to impossible. She had received some money from Reginald de Cröy and Monsieur Capiau, but the men who had been sent to her regularly since Monsieur Capiau's first appearance all had hearty appetites. Resources were at the breaking point. With a glance at the calendar she saw it was December 4, her birthday. With a pang, she realized that it would be the first year she had not received letters from Mother, Flo, Lil, Jack, and Eddy. She swallowed.

Jack growled softly, and she looked out the window. Two men were approaching the walkway. Bracing herself, she smoothed her hair, patted the dog, and went out into the hall to await their knock.

Although most of the men sent to the school only stayed one or two nights, some of them stayed longer. As Edith watched these two approach, she wondered how long she would need to provide them with shelter. When soldiers who were ill came to her, they were nursed right alongside German patients. Many of the nurses in the school were unaware of what was going on. All they saw were extra patients—bandaged, limping, and joking patients.

To recuperating soldiers, as well as to idle men, the Café Chez Jules situated right next to the school was a favorite gathering place. It served watered-down wine, and at its tables the men played cards, chatted, and lounged. Even if the Germans were not yet suspicious, Edith knew word had quickly spread around the Belgian neighborhood that Allied soldiers were hiding in the Rue de la Culture.

Once again, as she had done so often, Edith opened the door. A short, thickset man looked Edith full in the face.

"My name is Captain Tunmore, sole survivor of the First Battalion of the Norfolk Regiment." He spoke with a heavy English accent.

"And this," Captain Tunmore went on, indicating the man at his side, "is Private Lewis of the Cheshire Regiment. Password 'yorc.' We're both looking to get across the border."

Edith shook their hands.

The men were bewildered that this small, frail-looking lady whose hand totally disappeared in their grasp was rumored to be so tough.

Captain Tunmore, noting a picture on the wall, remarked, "Hey, that's Norwich Cathedral!"

"Do you know Norwich?" Edith asked.

"It's my home. I was born on its outskirts."

Edith took another look at the man. The fact that he said he was Norfolk born gave her, for just a small moment, the feeling that she was touching Swardeston, that she was looking into her mother's face.

"Well, gentlemen," she said with a smile, "I'm afraid you'll have to spend Christmas here with us as there is no guide to take you until after the twenty-fifth."

Captain Tunmore and Private Lewis had come without identity cards. Edith, consequently, took photographs of the men herself and had one of her contacts in the Resistance make identity cards for them. After Christmas, she arranged for them to travel toward Antwerp in a wagon. Unfortunately, they were discovered and barely made it back safely to the clinic a few days later. Edith decided she must guide them out of Brussels herself.

"Gentlemen, be ready at dawn tomorrow. I'll take you to the Louvain road. From there you're on your own."

At daybreak, with Edith in the lead and the men following at a discreet distance, the trio made their way to a road outside of Brussels. Once there, Edith passed the soldiers a packet of food and an envelope of money.

"In case you need to bribe someone. Or in case you get a chance to use the railway," she said. Shaking their hands once again, she turned and disappeared into the mist.

On the walk back, Edith reminisced about how she had walked these very paths with the François children. It now seemed ages ago that they had frolicked about her, collecting insects, drawing, running, and pulling at her arm to come and see some plant they had found. Now she understood that God, in his infinite wisdom, had used that time to intimately acquaint her with this area. How very strange providence was! At the time she had sometimes felt, although she loved the children dearly, that her task was unimportant—trivial perhaps. Yet it had equipped her for the role she now played. Smiling to herself she thought, *Why am I surprised? After all, doesn't the Bible say that it is important to be faithful over a few things?*

A noise to her left interrupted her reverie, and she slowed down. A German guard suddenly loomed next to her.

"*Halt! Papieren, bitte*—Stop! Papers, please."

Silently she took them out and waited. He waved her on after a moment, and she resumed her way. *What would her father have thought about these activities?* she wondered.

"Out so early, my Edith?" she imagined him asking.

"Yes, Father. Just a little matter of helping some soldiers escape to the front lines. If they are found, you see, they'll be sent to an internment camp somewhere, or they might be shot."

"What about you, my Edith?"

"Oh, don't worry about me, I'll be fine. And besides, what else can I do? These men, these refugee soldiers, Father, they just come to me. They arrive on my doorstep and look so helpless, so afraid that I will turn them away."

"Well, my Edith, you are doing right. Remember the words of the Lord Jesus, child: 'I was thirsty and ye gave me drink: I was a stranger, and ye took me in.'"

"I remember, Father. I remember."

"And in the end . . . in the end, Edith, He will say, 'Come, ye blessed of my Father, inherit the kingdom prepared for you from the foundation of the world.'"

"I know, Father."

Throughout the spring of 1915, Edith continued to rise early on the mornings that soldiers were to leave for the frontier. English, French, and Belgians—they were all men eager to leave so that they could help the Allies. Between five and seven in the morning, she would accompany the men to the planned rendezvous point with the next guide, generally a tramway terminus or a point in some street.

Arriving back after one such venture, in the early days of March, she found Elisabeth waiting for her in her office with a very guilty-looking Pauline and José at her side.

"What is the trouble?" Edith asked as she took off her coat.

"Would you like to tell her, or shall I?" Elisabeth's voice was angry.

José shuffled his feet but he met Edith's gaze. Then he spoke. "I encouraged all the families on Rue Darwin to set their alarm clocks at the same time. I told them to set it for six o'clock in the morning, the time I knew a single patrol would be passing."

He stopped. Edith sighed.

"And," she encouraged, "what happened?"

"Well, when all the alarms went off at the same time, the soldier jumped a mile into the air. You should have seen—"

"Was anyone hurt?" Edith interrupted him.

"No, no one," Pauline took over. "Everyone only let their alarms ring for five seconds exactly. After that they shut them off at the same time. It was deathly quiet in the streets, and all the people watched the silly soldier through their curtains as he looked behind him and around corners and pointed his silly rifle at nothing. We laughed so hard."

Edith sat down. "Do you have any idea what could have happened if that soldier had shot up at a window? Or if he had kicked open a door and . . . "

She paused. They really had no idea about the seriousness of the times in which they were living. She sighed again and went on. Pauline looked down at the floor, and José appeared fascinated with the wall.

"You ought to know better than anyone, José, how dangerous it was what you did. After all, you have come with me many times to help soldiers find their way through and out of Brussels so that they can escape to safety. War is not a game."

After they left her office thoroughly chastened, Edith sat down at her desk, put her head into her hands, and wept. Childhood seemed such a long way off, and the Germans were stealing much more than blackberry pie.

29

THE VALLEY OF THE SHADOW

March 11, 1915

Dear Eddy:

Remember when we were young, and life was fresh and beautiful, and the country so desirable and sweet? Remember the things we spoke of—the great things we would do?

Life is becoming more difficult here as the days go on. Just last week the Belgian nurses at St-Gilles Hospital were replaced by Germans. I've taken in as many of these girls as I had beds for, even though it adds a strain to my already meager budget. No more ice cream and cake, I suppose! Just joking! I was able to find jobs for some of them in the Brussels public schools.

Marie Depage has left for America on the Lusitania. *She is to solicit funds for war relief. It was hard to say good-bye. She has been such a dear friend, and I shall miss our talks together in the next while. Her husband (remember the ogre doctor Antoine Depage?) has set up a field hospital at La Panne. He is a good man, just has a bit of a temper.*

The once bustling streets here are quiet. So are the people who were once so gay and communicative. No one speaks to his neighbor on the tram anymore for he might be a spy. Besides, what news is there to tell, and who has the heart for gossip, and what fashions are there to speak of? There is great poverty, and it would be much worse but for the Americans who have taken it on themselves to provide the chief necessities of life. Even the pigeons look lean. But I am a looker-on after all, for it is not my country whose soil is desecrated and whose sacred places are laid waste. I can only feel the deep and tender pity of a friend within the gates.

A new nursing school to replace this one is being built only some ten minutes away from here on Rue de Bruxelles. It will be larger and better equipped than this one. As a result of the British blockade, there is considerable unemployment here, and workmen are easy to get right now. We rather fear, though, that soon these men will be deported to Germany.

A few days ago, I took ten nurses by train to Antwerp so that they might set up a clinic of sorts. That city has been ravaged terribly. There are multitudes of wounded from the Yser. I took the nurses to a private lodging house and settled them in. After this I said my farewells, hugged them, and began to walk back to the train station. Outside the house, suddenly overcome, I dropped down to my knees on the Flanders soil, muddy though it was. Spontaneously several girls ran out of the house and knelt with me. I had begun to recite the twenty-third psalm, and they joined in. In the distance, we could hear cannons, but our voices were strong as we lifted prayer to our Redeemer God. "Yea, though I walk through the valley of the shadow of death, I will fear no evil: for thou art with me; thy rod and thy staff they comfort me."

There are many things to do, and I am helping in a way I may not describe to you now. Indeed, there are many things I may not *write until we are free again. Do you think you could find out any news of the soldiers on the enclosed list? They are relatives of the girls here and fighting on the front.*

The last letter from Mother was dated January 22. If this reaches you, will you send her a line to say all is well here? She is naturally very anxious, and I do not know whether she gets my letters. There are not many opportunities of sending.

May God keep you.

Your loving cousin,
Edith Cavell

A few months later, as Edith was letting Jack out for a romp in the potato field across from the school, two men approached her from the direction of Rue Darwin. It had always amused Edith that the street adjoining Rue de la Culture was named Rue Darwin. The street could not help it, but every time she passed it she thought of lying and deceit.

"Pardon me, Madame," said one of the men, a well-dressed Englishman who showed all his teeth when he spoke. "We are looking for a place to hide until we can cross the frontier."

The second gentleman, a very tall fellow, nodded affably and stooped to stroke Jack. Totally out of character, the dog whined at the man's touch.

The encounter startled Edith. She had never been approached for help in broad daylight outside of her office. The workers in the potato field peered up at them as they weeded and hoed. For a moment she was undecided. Then she shrugged. After all, matters were in God's hands.

"Please follow me, gentlemen," she said.

The Englishman left for Holland the next day with a trusted guide, but the second man, Monsieur Gaston Quien, pleaded sick and stayed in the clinic. Funny, complimentary, and full of stories, he was soon immensely popular with the nurses. Pauline and Léonie, the cook's daughter, promptly fell in love with him.

"The German police are looking for me," he told an enraptured Pauline as they companionably sat on one of the school's many staircases. "But I have given them the slip many times and will do so again. I escaped from a prisoner-of-war camp by cutting barbed wire with a nail file. It was very cold outside, but—" and he looked at her tenderly, "my heart was warm. It was very likely preparing for the moment when I would see you."

Pauline giggled, and his hands reached out to encircle her waist.

"Monsieur Quien," Elisabeth's voice cut in above them, as she descended from the stairs, "should you not be lying down in bed, ill as you are?"

He stood up and bowed. "Ah, the beautiful Mademoiselle Wilkins," he said. "You remind me of my mother, rest her soul, who was always greatly concerned about my health."

"Pauline," Elisabeth said, "there's dusting to be done upstairs in room three. Please see to it."

Later, in Edith's office, Elisabeth vented her anger and her worry.

"The man's not to be trusted, Edith," she said. "Get him out of here. He's lollygagged about the halls for the last two weeks, and he's kissed I don't know how many of the nurses after paying them all sorts of silly compliments. Cook's Léonie is absolutely besotted by him, and Pauline . . . "

She stopped and sighed. Edith put an arm about her.

"Never mind, Elisabeth," she said. "There's another group leaving tomorrow, and I shall put it to him that he must either go with them or leave here for another lodging.

"Yes, do so," Elisabeth responded, immensely relieved, "for I won't sleep well until he's gone."

"Personally," Edith said, looking out the window across at the potato field, "I am more concerned about the workers there. I am sure that a few of them study the school far more than necessary."

Elisabeth came and stood next to her. "Why not give it up?" she whispered. "You said yourself, there are other houses where the guides take the men when we are full up."

"Yes," Edith whispered back. "But you see, then I would be turning them away, and that is precisely what I cannot do."

To their consternation, they saw a German officer approach the door at that very moment. He rang the bell and a moment later was shown into Edith's office by the portress.

"*Guten mittag*—good afternoon," he said.

"How can I help you, sir?" Edith replied, not bothering with the formalities of greeting.

"I have a son," the man said, all the while taking in the room carefully. "And he is *krank*—sick. I wonder, can he be admitted into one of your rooms?"

"*Nein*—no," Edith replied softly but firmly. "My rooms, you understand, are presently all full." She neglected to say that they were full because five English soldiers were sleeping in one of the wards.

"*Danke*—thank you," the officer responded, smartly clicking the heels of his polished boots together and saluting. "Then I will leave you."

After he left, Edith and Elisabeth sat down. Grinning weakly at one another with nervous relief, they did not speak for several minutes. Then a knock at the door made them jump to their feet again. It was Jacqueline.

"Can I speak to you for a minute?" she asked.

"Surely," Edith said, "Come in please and shut the door behind you."

"I have to tell you," Jacqueline said, "that I do not trust Monsieur Quien. This morning when I was out running errands, I saw him in a side street talking to a German officer."

Elisabeth and Edith exchanged a sharp glance.

"Yes," Edith said, "it's definitely time for Monsieur Quien to go. I will speak to him directly."

30

UNDER SURVEILLANCE

1915

Like a bad penny, Quien turned up again in July. He knocked at the clinic's door one day and told an astonished Edith that he had been drafted by the French Intelligence Service and that he needed a place to stay while he was working for them.

"I'm sorry, Monsieur Quien," she said, "but you will have to find different lodgings."

He smirked down at her from his six-foot-four height, but she did not budge. Eventually he left, turning a few times while walking down the street to look back at the school.

Edith was sure Monsieur Quien had seen much of what was going on in the clinic. Probably more than enough to condemn her. But if he were a spy, how was she to know that there were no other spies in the motley collection of men who took shelter here almost every day? Back in her office she sat down, resting her head in her hands. "Oh, Lord," she prayed, "make me humble. Make me trust you fully."

A little later, calm and composed, Edith told Elisabeth, "I am going out to check on the progress of the new school."

A few minutes after she left, the German secret police in the person of a Detective Otto Mayer came to call at the clinic. When Elisabeth opened the door, she did not realize the man was a German.

"Have you any left?" he asked her.

She supposed he meant nurses, as there were frequently inquiries for nursing help.

"No, none," she promptly replied.

"What!" he exclaimed, "No more Tommies?"

"I don't know what you mean!" a shocked Elisabeth exclaimed.

Detective Mayer lifted the lapel of his coat, and Elisabeth saw a badge—the badge of the secret police. Nevertheless, she firmly repeated what she had just said.

"I don't know what you mean."

"No?"

"No, sir. But if you have anything to discuss, you had better come in."

Elisabeth calmly led the way into Edith's office. Closing the door behind her, she smiled at the man. "Now, what exactly is it you want?"

"Oh, come now, Sister," he said, "you know what I want. The school has been hiding soldiers and Belgian men of military age for quite some time now. Everyone in the neighborhood knows it. Did you think we would be so stupid as to overlook your little facility?"

"I don't know what you are talking about," Elisabeth maintained. "But perhaps you would like to check our records?"

She pointed toward Edith's desk. It was stacked full of papers. Elisabeth knew the papers were innocuous, dealing with food, rations, and the running of the school.

"Hmm." Detective Mayer rifled through the papers for sometime but could find nothing incriminating.

"Would you like to visit the wards now?" Elisabeth asked.

"Yes, I would," he answered with grim formality.

Elisabeth led him up the stairs and to the men's ward.

"Please feel free to question the patients," she encouraged, knowing all of them were Germans.

Behind his back, however, she signaled Jacqueline and mouthed, "Police. Tell José."

Jacqueline nodded ever so slightly and disappeared.

Within moments, José had alerted the four Belgians who were currently lodging in the school. While Elisabeth kept the German police officer occupied, the fugitives slipped out the basement door into the garden and from there onto a neighboring lot.

After some time in the men's ward, Elisabeth asked the detective, "Are you satisfied, or is there something else?"

He looked up from the medical chart he was reading. "I want to see their papers," he snapped. "I want to see all the hospital papers."

Jacqueline reappeared and smiled at Elisabeth. Elisabeth smiled back, but her smile faded as she suddenly realized that the man might search Edith's private rooms as well.

"Has the patient in room five had his treatment yet?" Elisabeth shot the question at Jacqueline, winking at her as she did so.

"In room . . . ?" Jacqueline hesitated, puzzled for a moment, but then rallied. "No, he hasn't."

"Well, then I must see to that immediately." Elisabeth turned back to the officer. "You understand that work must go on."

Slipping out of the ward, she hurried to Edith's room, quickly gathering all the papers she could see. There was really no place to hide anything except in the lavatory. She ran back into the hall, opened the door of the water closet, and dropped the little bundle of papers down the toilet. Then she replaced the cover on the cistern. A moment later she walked down the hall again, almost bumping into Detective Mayer.

"Where are Matron Cavell's rooms?"

She turned and led him there. He looked around and opened some drawers but could find nothing incriminating.

"Don't imagine that I'm satisfied," he growled. "I'll be back."

An hour later, Edith returned. Elisabeth lost no time in telling her what had happened. "Please, Edith," she counseled, "we have to stop helping men now. Obviously the German police know what we are doing and they will not stop until . . . until they arrest you."

"I cannot stop," Edith sighed. "You know I cannot."

A few days later, Princess de Cröy came to the clinic. It was the first time she and Edith met, though for months they had been working with the same men.

"Your dog is *tres grand*—very big," she said.

"He won't hurt you," Edith said and smiled. To herself she chuckled as she thought, *Flo and Lil will never believe me when I tell them that a princess sat across from me in my office in the middle of the war and chatted about a dog.*

"I'm sorry," Edith said, "but you should not stay long, as the house is being watched continually. I'm afraid that I'm under suspicion. Those men you see through the window out in the field across the road . . . they have been there for some time now. They do little work in the field but watch us without stopping. And the German police have called—twice actually. The first time I was not in. The second time they took Elisabeth Wilkins away for questioning. She came back unharmed. They also searched the building, but before their search I was able to destroy any evidence I had on paper, and they went away dissatisfied. Nevertheless . . . " She stopped and sighed.

"I know the danger is increasing," the princess agreed. "And I am afraid our work must stop. Actually, that is what I came to tell you. We too have had search parties at the chateau. We dare not take any more men."

Edith nodded wearily. "When the Germans came the second time, I threw my papers into the grate, poured alcohol over them, and set them alight. Now all my records are gone, so how shall I explain the use of his money to Dr. Depage?" She passed her hand over her forehead and looked at the princess uneasily.

"Don't let that worry you," the princess responded immediately. "If we all come through this alive, I will be your witness. But it underlines the fact that we really and truly must stop."

A look of relief crept into Edith's face. But then, after a moment, she asked, "Are there any more men that need help?"

"Thirty more. Louise found them in the woods and fields near Cambrai."

"In that case we cannot quite stop yet. Because if one of those men were shot, it would be on our conscience. But now you must leave at once. Listen carefully to my instructions so that you will be able to get away safely."

The princess sat quietly as Edith explained.

"Go to the end of this road. There is a shop there. Look in the shop's window for a moment. It will reflect the street behind you. When you are sure there is no one there, turn quickly down the road on the left until you come to a pastry shop. This shop is right in front of the tram station. Hesitate at the shop as though you meant to enter it until you hear the bell of the approaching tram. When it is there, you must turn immediately and run for the tram and jump onto it, not minding which direction you go in. Will you promise me to do this?"

"I promise." Princess de Cröy walked up to Edith and opened her arms.

"You are my sister," she said, "and I love you."

Edith was moved by the embrace, and her tears began to flow as the princess whispered, "I was so very sorry to hear of Marie Depage's death on the *Lusitania*. I know that you were good friends."

A choked "thank you" was all Edith could manage. A moment later she watched from her window as the small figure of the princess disappeared down the road.

31

THE PRICE OF FREEDOM

More fugitives came. It did not matter that Elisabeth pleaded with Edith to refrain from harboring them, implored her to ask permission to return to England or, at the very least, to go into hiding. Edith would not listen.

Nine soldiers, the first of the thirty who had been hiding near Cambrai, were put into the back room on the first floor. They had only been at the school a few hours when the German police arrived. Elisabeth immediately took the soldiers out the back door into the garden. From there they climbed over a stone wall and ran to the vacant house next to the school.

Meanwhile, Edith's office was turned upside down. Her Norwich picture was torn from the wall, cups and saucers were smashed on the ground, floor boards were pried loose, and books were thrown helter-skelter about the room. Then the police left as suddenly as they had come, leaving an inspector behind to guard. He sat in the dining room puffing on a cigar. With knowing looks at the heavy-set man, the nurses calculated that he would likely fall asleep before midnight. He did.

In the dead of night, José guided four of the refugees to another address, and Pauline walked the remaining five outside of the city limits. Maria, one of the nurses, volunteered to stay up all night and watch at the window to see if any more refugees would approach the house. Jacqueline, unable to sleep, got up and sat beside her.

Around midnight, three shadowy figures approached. They were English. Maria instantly ran down the stairs to the front door. Opening it as quietly as she could, she waved her white handkerchief at them and put her finger on her lips. Then she pointed to their shoes and whispered, "*La Boche*—a German," nodding her head toward the front room. They understood, took off their shoes, and followed Maria to a large linen cupboard. She gestured for them to hide inside the closet and then went to tell Edith what had happened. She found Edith fully dressed in her blue uniform and hat, kneeling by her bed in prayer.

"Madame!" Maria's whisper was urgent. "Three more men came, Madame! What shall we do?"

Edith slowly got up. Smoothing down the wrinkles in her skirt, she deliberated for a few moments. Then, putting on her coat, she walked into the hall and let the men out of the closet, indicating that they should follow her. Vanishing into the dark night, she took them on a six-kilometer hike to another safe address. The German guard did not hear her come back, and at seven o'clock the following morning he left. The entire building suddenly breathed more easily.

While the occupation and fighting continued, so did the school's move to its new building. One day, coming back from helping move furniture to the new facility, José shouted, "Madame! Madame!" as he ran into the clinic.

Out of breath, he sat down for a moment on an upturned packing crate. Edith patted him on the shoulder and was about to fetch him a glass of water when he began to weep.

"Monsieur Baucq has been arrested, Madame! They found four thousand copies of *La Libre Belgique*—our freedom paper. He was taken to the prison at St-Gilles."

Edith sat down on another crate and looked at him. "Do not worry, José," she said softly. "Just go on with the moving. You are, and always have been, a tremendous help to me."

"Oh, Madame," he said awkwardly, "you have been like a mother."

He wiped his eyes but did not go back to the new school. Instead, he and the remaining nurses loitered about, torn between carrying something else over to the new building and staying with Edith, who calmly went on packing.

An hour passed, and it began to seem as if nothing would happen. Then an automobile drove down Rue de la Culture. It stopped at number 149. Two men got out, one of whom was Detective Mayer. Marching up the walkway, they entered the house. When the detective saw the girls and José in the front room, he ordered them not to move. He and his officers then strode into Edith's office, reappearing minutes later with Edith between them.

José and the girls jumped up in alarm.

As the men pushed Edith toward the door, she smiled at the desolate little group. "Don't be so sad, my children," she said. "Everything will be all right. I'll be back soon."

Then the men dragged her down the walk and into the car. As it drove away, Pauline ran after it, tripping in her haste and skinning a knee. The workers in the potato field stared, and the men drinking wine at Café Chez Jules went on drinking.

Later that day, Elisabeth Wilkins was arrested again. Before nightfall, however, she was released.

Edith was not so fortunate. She was detained, and the next day Grace received a letter from her.

August 6, 1915

My dearest Grace:

I do hope you are not worrying about me. Tell everybody that I am quite all right. I suppose, from what I have heard, I shall be questioned one of these days, and when they have got all they want I shall know what they mean to do with me. There are numerous prisoners here, and there is no chance of being lonely. We can buy food at the canteen, but I should be glad to have one of our red blankets, a serviette, cup, fork, spoon, and plate—not one of the best ones—also one or two towels and my toothbrush, and in a day or two some clean linen. I am afraid you will not be able to come and see me at present. But you can write—only your letter will be read. Is Sister Wilkins free? I have been thinking of her ever since last night. Tell them to go on with the move. If Sister White is there, she will know how to arrange everything. Is Jack sad? Please pat him for me and tell him I will be back soon. The day is rather long. So, please send me a book, a little embroidery, my nail scissors, and only a very few other things, as I have no place to put them. I will write again when there is something to tell. Don't worry—we must hope for the best.

Please tell the girls thank you for the lovely flowers they have sent. Tell them all to go on as usual, and let us place our trust in him who is worthy of our praise.

> *Your foster mother who loves you very much,*
> *Edith Cavell*

32

More Than a Patriot

August-October 1915

After a few days at the police station, Edith was transferred to St-Gilles. Her cell was not large. She did not complain, but her heart sighed as she stood in the small room and saw that through the only window—a window nearly two meters above the floor—she would not even be able to glimpse sky. The cot, which folded out to a bed at night, doubled as a table in the day. A wooden stool and a little cupboard in the corner completed the furniture. Neatly and lovingly, she placed her Bible in the cupboard next to her embroidery. For a moment she thought how nice it would be if she had her picture of Swardeston to hang on the bleak wall.

Every now and then eyes gleamed at her through a rectangular peephole in the door. Through this hole the guard was able to observe her day and night.

As the days passed, Edith's life fell into a new routine. Twice a week she was permitted to walk for half an hour in a tiny *préau,* a courtyard located within the center of the prison. A guard watched her from the door and warned her to keep walking until her time was up. Although the meager prison ration could be supplemented with food from the outside, Edith refused this privilege except on Sundays. On this day José brought in a special basket with meat and vegetables in the lower compartment and pudding in the top. She treasured the love that brought this basket. It made her remember the Sundays when she had been little—the Sundays she had carried containers of food to the poor in Swardeston.

"You must remember," her father had said, "that at some point in your life you might be at the receiving end. You might be reduced to such straits as to be glad of a cup of cold water. You might be sick, friendless, and alone somewhere where you will feel absolutely forsaken. But remember that you will never be so alone that God is not there."

Edith remembered and, although four bare walls stared at her, she knew that she was not alone.

There were repeated cross-examinations by the secret police. Detective Mayer and Herr Bergan, the chief of police, informed her time and again that other prisoners had confessed.

"We know that you have been helping soldiers by allowing them to stay at your clinic." Detective Mayer hammered away at her repeatedly. "We know you let them pose as patients; and we know that you gave them food and money."

Edith remained silent until, finally exhausted by the verbal attacks, she nodded. After all, what they said was true. It did not occur to her that they were bluffing, nor that they lied to her when they said that other prisoners had confessed.

As the interrogation continued, Herr Bergan leaned his face so close to hers that she could smell the onions he had eaten for lunch. "We also know that you have helped Belgian men reach enemy territory where they joined armies which fight against us." With his menacing face inches from her own, he said, "Do you realize that in hiding these men you have hindered the German cause and helped our enemies?"

"My aim has not been to assist your enemies but to help these men gain the frontier. Once across they were free to do what they liked."

"How many men have you helped get to the frontier?"

"About two hundred."

"Were all these men English?"

"Not all. Some were French, and others were Belgians."

"Were you not foolish to help the English? They are such an ungrateful people."

"No, they are not."

"How do you know?"

"Because some of them have written from England to thank me."

In the end, to the German officers' delight, Edith signed a confession. Because they had gotten all the information they needed to convict her, her captors allowed her to receive letters and communicate in a limited way with friends before she was brought to trial.

August 23, 1915

Dear Elisabeth:

I am sorry you had to wait so long for an answer. I have asked to see you but it may not be until after sentence. So do not try any

more. Just write all you want to know and I will reply on the first
possible occasion.

Many thanks for asking what I need. I should like a comb, a
little notepaper and some hankies—also my Imitatio Christi, *a*
little red book on the shelf in my bedroom, as well as my prayer book.
Tell Pauline to be a good girl. I hope José is well. My dear old Jack!
Please brush him sometimes and look after him. I am quite well and
more worried about the school than my own fate. Tell the girls to
work well and be tidy. Don't buy anything for me. I do very well on
what I have. My love to you, and please see that the nurses who are
supposed to write their exams are studying regularly.

Your dear friend,
Edith Cavell

In the last few years, there had always been urgent matters: ledgers to keep up, food supplies to be seen to, classes
to arrange, operations in which to assist, and, during the last
while, soldiers to hide. But now, alone in her cell, Edith rested.
She did some embroidery, walked about the cell reading Scrip-
tures out loud, and softly sang "Rock of Ages" as she lay on her
bed at night. She actually looked forward to having her small
meals handed to her by the jailer without having to worry
whether there was enough to go around. After all, there was
only herself—herself and God.

She made small notations in her prayer book and thought
deeply about what she was reading. "Into thy hands I com-
mend my spirit, for thou hast redeemed me, O Lord, thou
God of truth." Meditating on the words, she wondered, *Is
my spirit humble enough to rest in God's hands? Am I ready to give up
everything for my Lord?* She smoothed the folds of her nursing
uniform, stared at the cuffs that had once been much whiter,

and felt her starched collar and her cap. All these she still wore because she had been arrested in her uniform. But surely she was not a uniform. Surely she should not depend on a uniform. She was Edith—Edith Louisa Cavell, child of God and in his care.

In September, when Elisabeth Wilkins was at last granted permission to visit, Edith asked her to bring civilian clothes. The trial began the first week of October, and Edith wore a plain, dark blue dress. She looked fragile and petite with nothing to plead for her but her faith. The proceedings lasted two days—Thursday, October 7, and Friday, October 8. A day and a half later, Sunday, October 10, 1915, sentence was pronounced.

On the evening of the same day, Stirling Gahan, English chaplain at the legation in Brussels, found a penciled note on his desk when he returned from conducting an evening service. It was a message from Monsieur Le Seur, the pastor for the German soldiers, requesting that he visit an English woman in St-Gilles prison—a woman who was to be shot the next morning. Rev. Gahan put his coat back on and began the long walk to the prison.

It was cold outside, and a heavy rain was falling. Clutching his coat collar tightly around his neck, Rev. Gahan strode along as quickly as he could. Before long, rain dripped down his hat and ran into his collar. The streets were deserted. Families stayed indoors. It seemed that winter had come early.

When the minister reached St-Gilles, a guard permitted him to enter. Following the guard, his footsteps echoed hollowly along the corridors as he made his way through endless passages and past countless doors. Finally halting, the guard slipped a key into one of the doors. It opened with a creak, and Rev. Gahan entered cell number 23.

A woman rose from the metal cot on which she had been lying. Tucking a dressing gown snugly about her, she smiled and held out her hand. "Good evening, Reverend Gahan. Thank you for coming."

He knew the woman because she had faithfully attended worship services. "Good evening, Miss Cavell."

It was difficult for Rev. Gahan to hide the shocked expression on his face at Edith's changed appearance. She had always been tiny and slender, but the last ten weeks of imprisonment had caused her to lose much weight. She noted his discomfort on her behalf and hastened to reassure him.

"I am well," she said, and with the air of a hostess invited him to take off his coat and to sit down.

He sat on the stool, and Edith sat on the edge of the cot.

"I am most unhappy about the outcome of the trial," Rev. Gahan said.

"I had not expected it," she answered simply, "but I am extremely grateful to my God and Father for the weeks of rest which I have had."

He nodded and waited for her to continue.

She folded her hands in her lap and looked at him calmly. "During this time I have been able to read and reflect."

A guard walked by in the hall. The sound of his heavy boots rang through the cell. Unperturbed, Edith continued, her gray eyes shining.

"They have been kind to me here. I have no fear or shrinking. I have seen death so often that it is not fearful or strange to me. And now, standing in view of God and eternity, I realize that patriotism is not enough. I must have no hatred or bitterness toward anyone."

Rev. Gahan drew his prayer book from his pocket. Standing up, he walked toward the cot. "Shall we pray together?"

She nodded and stood up as well. Then they knelt, side by side, in front of the cot. And the cell became a sanctuary.

After the prayer, they stood, and Rev. Gahan placed the Communion vessels he had taken with him on the bed. They partook of the Lord's Supper together.

Edith was very quiet and listened intently as the words of the sacrament were read—words of assurance and pardon, words of eternal life.

Then the minister softly began to recite the words of the last verse of the hymn "Abide with Me." Edith joined him, and they half-spoke, half-sang together most of the well-known song.

Swift to its close ebbs out life's little day;
Earth's joys grow dim, its glories pass away;
Change and decay in all around I see;
O, thou who changest not, abide with me.

They were quiet a few moments after that, and then, as the hour he had been allotted by the guard drew to a close, Rev. Gahan stood up and put his coat back on.

Edith took out a packet of letters she had written earlier that evening. "Please give these to Elisabeth so that they can be sent out," she asked.

He took them. Not wishing to leave but knowing that there was no choice, he quietly said, "I had better go as you must rest."

A wry smile touched her mouth. "Yes, I have to be up at five a.m."

"Good-bye," he said, his voice thick with sorrow and admiration.

"We shall meet again," she replied. Unflinchingly she looked into his eyes before turning to walk back to her cot. Her back was straight.

Once more Rev. Gahan followed the guard down the long corridors of the prison. It was still raining out when he reached the door.

Before dawn, on October 12, 1915, Edith Cavell was taken to Tir National, the Brussels firing range. A Lutheran pastor was present. He was allowed to speak a few words with Edith and bestow a blessing.

"The grace of our Lord Jesus Christ and the love of God and the communion of the Holy Spirit be with you forever," he said.

Standing erect and composed, Edith said, "Ask Mr. Gahan to tell my loved ones later on that my soul, I believe, is safe and that I am glad to die for my country."

A company of eight soldiers faced Edith, raised their guns, and waited for the command. "Fire!"

HISTORICAL NOTE

Edith's death was not the warning to the Allies the Germans meant it to be. Within days of her shooting, Edith Cavell had become a heroine, a martyr who had given her life for others. Her execution strengthened Allied morale, and recruitment doubled for eight weeks after her death was announced.

Four years later, on May 17, 1919, her body was exhumed. Guarded by the Belgian army, it was taken to Ostend and from there, guarded by the Royal British Navy, shipped across the channel back to England. There, her body was placed on a train, which had been draped and painted black, and carried to London. Word was passed down the line, "Edith Cavell is home." The streets were crowded with soldiers and civilians alike, and along the Thames embankment thousands of men, women, and children watched as the casket, covered with a Union Jack as well as with an immense cross of red and white carnations, passed by. No one spoke as the coffin was carried into Westminster Abbey. Inside the abbey, a lengthy service concluded with the hymn "Abide with Me." Later, the body was reburied near her earthly home in Norwich Cathedral.

Posthumous honors were also conferred on Edith. The Cross of the Order of Leopold was bestowed by King Albert of Belgium. The Belgian government gave *La Croix*

Cívique—the Civilian Cross. France made her a Chevalier of the Legion of Honor. But all these things were trifles compared with what had already been bestowed on her by Jesus—the crown of life.

Author's Note

Edith Cavell was a remarkable woman. Content to be obscure, she worked hard and lived humbly. But those virtues in and of themselves are not enough to make one remarkable. Surely there have been tens of millions of obscure women who worked hard and lived humbly. But the main reason we should read about and reflect upon the life of Edith Cavell is that she was a godly woman and, therefore, a godly historical example. The Bible instructs us to teach our children about such historical examples. Psalm 78:4 reads: "We will not hide them from their children, but tell to the coming generation the glorious deeds of the Lord and his might, and the wonders that he has done." At a time in history when examples of godly women are few and far between, much needed strength and encouragement can be drawn from the life of this lady who put all her trust in Jesus Christ, her Savior.

The dates and main characters portrayed in this book are all fairly accurate. Nevertheless, writing a biography remains a tricky business. Although I have tried to gauge Edith's thoughts and motivations by reading copiously about her, her family, and her times, there were certain gaps that needed filling. Consequently, a few scenes and conversations truly fall within the realm of historical fiction, which is, after all, what this book is—a historical fiction. The blackberry pie incident, for example, although highly probable given Edith's exceptional desire in later life to speak the truth, I made up.

There is no doubt that Edith was blessed with loving parents who instructed her in Bible knowledge and who were examples to her of godly living. Instilled with a desire to please her Creator God, Edith Cavell lived what she professed. In a seemingly hopeless situation, she persevered and did not shun the victor's crown. She was a gift given by God to his Son Jesus Christ and, as such, saved for eternal life.

GLOSSARY

battledore and shuttlecock: game from which badminton was developed

Belgian National Anthem—Brabançonne: The anthem's first two lines are "O dear Belgium, O holy land of our fathers, Our souls and hearts are dedicated to you." Part of the refrain reads "For king, for freedom, and for justice."

bronchopneumonia: inflammation of the bronchii (two main branches of the trachea) and lungs.

busbies: tall, fur hats with baglike ornaments hanging from the top over the right side

chilblains: inflammation of the hands and feet caused by exposure to cold and moisture

common: tract of land owned or used jointly by the members of a community

concierge: person who has charge of the entrance of a building

curate: clergyman employed as assistant of a vicar

fichu: woman's kerchief, generally triangular in shape, for wearing about the neck with the ends drawn together or crossed

French window: window extending to the floor, with doors usable as entrance or exit

hedge flowers: varieties of European herbs having calyxes resembling a helmet

Imitatio Christi—*Imitation of Christ,* a book by Thomas á Kempis written to promote personal piety

landau: four-wheeled, two-seated carriage

livery: distinctive dress worn by a member of a company, guild, or special household

loge: booth in a theater or opera house

Meachin: This English sergeant made it safely back to England, returned to the front, and gained the D.C.M. (Distinguished Conduct Medal).

mobilize: to assemble men of military age into readiness for battle

Nightingale, Florence: English nurse and hospital reformer who lived from 1820 to 1910

Ostend: seaport in northwest Belgium

pince-nez: pair of glasses with a spring to clip to the nose

rostrum: pulpit or raised platform

Ruskin, John: English author, art critic, and social reformer (1819–1900)

sabots: wooden shoes, klompen

Sunday school: Although the Sunday school was an old religious institution, there was a revived interest in it during the 1800s. It often also served as a day school, and many young people got their education in these institutions.

surreptitiously: stealthily, furtively

Thomas à Kempis: a German priest and author (1380–1471)

Tommy: nickname for a British soldier

Tredegar House: preliminary training school for nurses at the London Hospital, opened in 1896

trench: long, narrow ditch, especially dug by troops to stand in and be sheltered from enemy's fire

Tunmore: British sergeant from Norfolk, who, after Edith left him, managed to get within three miles of the Dutch frontier. Here all the pedestrians had to cross over on a bridge. It was heavily guarded. He and Private Lewis, his companion, used the money Edith had given them to bribe a bargeman, who lent them his boat in which they slipped across successfully. Once on the other side, they managed to make it into Holland without incident.

Uhlan: lancer in a heavy German cavalry unit

vaulted lierne: ornamental arched structure on a ceiling or roof

water closet: toilet

TIMELINE

1837   Victoria becomes Queen of England

1840   Queen Victoria marries Prince Albert

1854–1856   Crimean War

1859   Darwin's *The Origin of Species* is published

1861–1865   United States Civil War

1865   Edith Cavell is born

              William Booth begins preaching career in London

              Lewis Carroll's *Alice in Wonderland* is published

1867   Cavells move into their own house

1876   Alexander Graham Bell invents the telephone

1878   Electric street lights introduced in London

1879   Edith writes to the bishop of Norwich

1884   Edith goes to Laurel Court

1887   Queen Victoria's Golden Jubilee

1888   London Girls' Match Strike

1890   Edith recommended for a post in Brussels with the
              Francois family

              Global flu epidemics

1895   Edith returns to England to nurse her father

1896   Edith accepted at Fountains Fever Hospital as a nursing
              student

              First modern Olympics

1897   Typhoid fever epidemic in Maidstone

1899–1902 Boer War in South Africa

1901   Queen Victoria dies; Edward VII begins reign

1906   Edith goes to work in the Manchester area for the Queen's District Nursing Homes

1907   Edith returns to Brussels to head a nurses' training program

1912   *Titanic* sinks

1914   World War I begins

               Lusitania sinks

1915   Edith arrested by the Germans

BIBLIOGRAPHY

á Kempis, Thomas. *The Imitation of Christ*. New York: Vintage Books, 1984.

Adam, George. *Treason and Tragedy*. London: Jonathan Cape, 1929.

Altick, Richard D. *Victorian People and Ideas*. New York: W.W. Norton & Company, Inc., 1973.

Bailey, Brian. *Villages of England*. New York: Harmony Books, 1984.

Clark-Kennedy, A. E. *Edith Cavell: Pioneer and Patriot*. London: Faber and Faber, 1965.

de Cröy, Princess Marie. *War Memories*. London: Macmillan, 1932.

Elkon, J. *Edith Cavell, Heroic Nurse*. New York: Julian Messner, Inc., 1962.

Grey, E. *Friend Within the Gates*. London: Constable & Co. Ltd., 1960.

Hart, Roger. *English Life in the Nineteenth Century*. London: Wayland Publishers, 1971.

Hibbert, Christopher. *The English—A Social History, 1066–1945*. London: Grafton Books, 1987.

Hoehling, A. A. *A Whisper of Eternity*. New York: Thomas Yoseloff, Inc., 1957.

Massie, Robert K. *Dreadnought*. New York: Ballantine, 1991.

McKown, Robin. *Heroic Nurse*. New York: G. P. Putnam's Sons, 1966.

Morris, E. W. *A History of the London Hospital*. London: Edward Arnold, 1910.

Priestly, J. B. *The Edwardians*. London: Heinemann, 1970.

Trevelyan, G. M. *Illustrated English Social History, Volume 4*. London: Longmans, Green and Co., 1942.

Vinton, Iris. *The Story of Edith Cavell.* New York: Grosset and Dunlop, 1959.

Whitlock, Brand. *Belgium Under German Occupation, Volume 1.* London: William Heinemann, 1919.

Wilkins, Frances. *Six Great Nurses.* London: Hamish Hamilton, 1962.

Christine Farenhorst, author and poet, is a columnist for *Reformed Perspective*, a contributing writer for *Christian Renewal*, and a reviewer for Christian Schools International. She is the author of *Wings Like a Dove*, *Amazing Stories from Times Past*, *The Great Escape*, *Suffer Annie Spence*, *The Letter Child*, and *Before My Mother's Womb*. As well, she has written a collection of poems, *You and I*, and has co-authored two church history textbooks for children. Christine and her husband, Anco, have five children, nineteen grandchildren, a dog, and ten chickens.